Ormeshadow

ALSO BY PRIYA SHARMA

All the Fabulous Beasts

ORMESHADOW

PRIYA SHARMA

A TOM DOHERTY ASSOCIATES BOOK

NEW YORK

ORMESHADOW

Cover design by Henry Sene Yee

Edited by Ellen Datlow

A Tor.com Book
Published by Tom Doherty Associates
120 Broadway
New York, NY 10271

www.tor.com

Tor® is a registered trademark of
Macmillan Publishing Group, LLC.

ISBN 978-1-250-24143-6 (ebook)
ISBN 978-1-250-24144-3 (trade paperback)

First Edition: October 2019

To my parents, Veronica and Krishan Sharma,
who both have a passion for stories

Ormeshadow

The Journey

THE ARGUMENT STARTED a good twenty miles from Ormeshadow. It was because of the old gallows.

The journey had started in the grand city of Bath.

"Why do we have to leave?" Gideon asked his father.

"Yes, John," his mother put in. "Explain to Gideon why we have to go."

"We're going to stay with my brother and his family in Ormeshadow."

"But—"

"Gideon, it's a long journey. Settle down, son."

"That's right," Clare added. "Let's not talk of it."

Those were the last words Gideon's parents spoke to one another until they reached the gallows. Gideon was used to his mother's obstinate silence, so it didn't bother him much despite their proximity in the crowded carriage. The flattened, threadbare cushions offered little comfort as they were thrown about.

Gideon felt his father's arm slide around his shoulders to steady him. "I'll show you the Orme when we get there."

"Orme?"

"It's the Old English word for worm or dragon."

"Dragons aren't real."

"Are you sure?"

In Bath there was lamplight and street theatre. There had been the great house with a library where his father worked for the old man. Living in Bath it was easy not to believe in dragons.

"So there *are* dragons?"

"There's a legend that a great dragon flew over the bay and then swooped down to cool herself in the sea. She crept along the shore and settled with her head resting on her folded forelegs. Smoke came from her nostrils. She was tired, shifting in the sunlight like an adder warming itself in the heather."

Once his father started a story his voice changed, like he was reading from a book within him. It lulled Gideon.

"The Orme slept for hundreds of years. Grass grew along her back. Most people forgot her. A village sprang up in her shadow and still she sleeps on."

"What do dragons look like?" Gideon imagined them to be ugly.

"She's a fierce beauty. Her scales are burnished copper, worn green at the edges. Her nostrils are darkened by fire. On her forehead the copper becomes a crown of bronze and gold. The Orme's belly and flanks are a lighter colour, the scales moving over each other like plates of armour."

"What about her eyes?"

"Purple, with black slits that open wide in the dark."

"How can they make fire and not be burnt?"

"It's in their hearts when they're angry or afraid and it spews out in torrents. Their insides are lined like furnaces to keep them from burning up in a rage. Their teeth are like elephant tusks."

The king had come to Bath once, to take the spa waters. A circus was brought from India for his entertainment. Acrobats flipped and turned. A boy climbed a levitating rope. Gideon loved the parading elephant best, with her flapping ears, but the iron manacles on her legs made him sad.

"Dragons have claws like giant scimitars."

The elephant had been ridden by a pretend sultan with a diadem, a curved blade hanging from his waist catching the torchlight.

"When will the Orme wake up?"

"When she's ready."

It was then that Gideon saw the gallows. He turned to his father, pointing. He wasn't allowed to attend the public hangings in Bath and if he happened to chance past one, he couldn't see for the deep, high crowds. There was jeering and roaring. A sense of spectacle. Here, in the silent emptiness, Gideon had an uninterrupted view.

Gideon's father made a face even though there was nothing to see but dead wood. "Don't look, son."

"Why shouldn't he look?" His mother's voice was contrary. "You fill his head with stupid stories and keep him ignorant of everything important."

"He's only a boy," John replied. "Life's full enough of heartaches, Clare." Gideon could see his father was embarrassed to be talking like this in front of strangers.

"The sooner he knows about them, the better."

The old woman opposite crossed herself. Her companion leaned forward, seeming to be glad at last of the opportunity to engage the Belmans in conversation. A battered Bible sat on his knee, proclaiming his faith.

"William Fletcher was the last man hanged here." The old man's face was as lined as his good book. "It was sixty years ago, before the magistrate's court was moved to Carrside. He was a famous pickpocket who specialised in linens."

The gallows were at a crossroads to confuse William Fletcher's thieving soul. Gideon imagined the wind playing with his long hair and ravens perched above his swinging corpse, waiting to be alone with him. The buckles on his shoes glinted dimly.

Clare stared down the God-fearing man.

"Was it right to hang a man for stealing some rich man's handkerchief to feed his children?"

"I doubt his motives were so pure." Gideon recognised that the man, just like his mother, was used to having the final say. "A thief is a thief and justice is justice. We'd all be safer if the law was as firm as it was back then."

The righteous man folded his hands on his Bible, resolute. Clare's eyes flashed a look that Gideon knew well. He wished he'd not drawn attention to the old gibbet.

"So those who have everything are able to keep down those who have nothing. You'd have us go back to when a magistrate could sentence a man to death for taking a scrap of cloth, when those he's stole from have a dozen more at home? Yet lords can take all they want at no cost to themselves, offer any woman an insult, dismiss a man after years of service . . ."

"Hush, Clare, please." John Belman reached across Gideon and laid a gentle hand on her arm. "Not now. Not like this."

The coach clattered past the gallows. When Gideon dared to glance at his mother she was staring from the window as if she could see William Fletcher still hanging there and wanted to burn the memory of his face in her mind forever.

~

They changed at The Swan at Carrside. The coachman

helped them untie their belongings from the roof of the coach, where they had been lashed down with heavy rope. All the family owned lay there by the road as they waited for the dogcart: a trunk buckled with leather straps, a carpet bag, and a tea chest. Everything else had been sold.

Not much with which to start a new life.

When the carter arrived he nodded at Gideon's father as though they knew each other. Smoke climbed from the pipe clenched in the man's teeth. He doffed his cap at Clare, but his gallantry didn't extend to helping her climb up onto the seat beside him. Gideon noticed, because men were always particular about being gallant toward his mother.

Gideon stretched out in the back with the luggage, bracing his feet against the trunk to steady himself. He rested against the carpetbag, and from this vantage point he had an uninterrupted view of the stars. The sky was clearer than it was at home, the moon brighter.

It was only when the cart jolted on the cobbles of a yard that Gideon knew they'd arrived at Ormesleep Farm. The baritone bark of an unseen dog confirmed it.

The farmhouse door was closed. A single candle glowed in the window, but it was too small to battle the darkness stretching out for miles around them. A moth struggled against the windowpane, seeking the salvation of the light. Nobody stirred within.

A dog, black with white flashes on its chest, came from the barn. Gideon put out his hand to stroke her. She could be the dog he'd always longed for, his first friend at Ormesleep, and she'd come when he called. Clare slapped his hand away.

"That's no pet. It's a working dog."

A second dog had come to inspect them, sniffing and growling.

The door remained closed. The carter drove away without a goodbye, not seeming to care if they were left out in the cold overnight. Clare clutched Gideon to her in her normal way, his back against her and her hand flat on his chest. It was the closest Gideon ever came to an embrace from her.

"Well?"

John knocked on the door.

"For heaven's sake, let me." Clare pushed him aside, rapping with her small, sharp fist. "Fine welcome this is."

The candle in the window moved and Gideon was startled by the face illuminated by the flame. It peered at them, all eyes and a cloud of golden hair, before receding. Then the door opened. A woman, in her nightgown and shawl, stood before them.

"Maud? I'm John." John proffered his hand. "Apologies for our lateness. We were held up at Flay. One of the horses lost a shoe."

"I'm sorry," Maud said as she drew them into the kitchen, "I thought you wouldn't come tonight after all."

She lit the lamps. They'd made smoky patches on the wall. Gideon slipped his hands into his mother's. For once she didn't pull away.

"Maud, this is my wife, Clare, and my son, Gideon." Then to them, "Come and meet my brother's wife, Maud."

"Thank you for taking us in." Clare nodded stiffly.

"You're very welcome!" Maud turned her large eyes on them. "Welcome, sister. I dare say you'll find it quiet here after living in Bath."

"I'll be glad of some peace."

An oak table and benches dominated the kitchen. Gideon ran his fingers over the tabletop, its surface worn smooth and carved out with names. His saw his father's name, *John Belman,* dug into the surface in crude letters, but it had been scored through with a line, gouged deep into the wood as if to erase it. Aunt Maud talked as she pulled a leg of meat from the crock and carved off slices.

"I've made a bed for Gideon down here." She pulled open a door. Inside was a closet, not a room, containing a low cot and not much else. Maud shrugged, embarrassed.

She handed out plates of cold meat and bread and

then turned to crouch in front of the cold fireplace. "I've sorted out the back bedroom for you."

"Maud, where's my brother?"

Maud's shoulders froze a fraction, then she started cleaning out the grate.

"At The Ship."

"What time will he be home?"

Maud's smile was brittle. "A man is master in his own home. He comes and goes as he pleases."

Gideon struggled with the tough lamb. Cold fat clung to it. He could see his father's face tensing, the muscles of his jaw standing up.

"Of course," John answered finally.

They finished their meal in silence.

A moth followed Gideon's candle into the closet. It settled on the candlestick as he set it down. Mottled brown and grey, it looked as delicate as an autumn leaf, at risk of burning up in its adoration of the flame.

First Morning

GIDEON'S SLEEP HAD BEEN restless. He woke to find himself bound up in the blankets. The darkness confused him. In Bath, light crept around the corners of the curtains with each new day. He'd hear the family who roomed above them; chairs scraping the floor and the tumble of feet.

This wasn't home. This was Ormesleep Farm.

The walls of the airless closet pressed in on him. The plaster smelt of mildew. He groped under the cot for his clothes and dressed.

Gideon opened the door. The ticking clock reassured him the world hadn't stopped. It was half past six. He realised he was hungry. He couldn't smell breakfast, but at least there was a fire. It crackled and spat, angry at being newly lit. There was a tin bath hung up on one wall and a dresser loaded with mismatched crockery against the other.

A floorboard creaked. He turned, expecting Aunt Maud, but found a dark man watching him.

"Uncle Thomas?" Gideon asked.

The man appraised him without a word. He sat at the head of the table, in the only chair in the kitchen. It was a piece of furniture fit for a mansion, not a farmhouse. Gideon hadn't noticed it the night before, being so tired.

The chair was high-backed, like a throne, carvings of fish twisted around the legs. The arms were finished with dragons, worn to a high shine by caressing hands.

The man himself was a lean, wiry version of Gideon's father. He wore a patched work jacket over a rough shirt. He seemed at great pains to be still, but his eyes were churning pools. Gideon expected him to spring up at any second.

"Uncle Thomas?" Gideon repeated.

Gideon was relieved to hear footfalls from the corridor off the kitchen that led to his parents' new bedroom.

"You're back then." Uncle Thomas picked up his cup and slurped his steaming tea.

"It's good to see you again after all this time, Thomas." Gideon felt his father's hand on his shoulder. "Gideon, meet your uncle."

"He looks like a Belman." Thomas put the cup down.

"Why would he look like anything else?"

Gideon was startled by his father's sharpness.

Gideon looked from one face to the other, their gazes locked, the same challenge in both pairs of eyes. His father was clean-shaven and straight-backed, while his uncle was stubbled and slouching. A different sort of man altogether.

The kitchen filled around them. It was Maud and Gideon's cousins. Charity, the baby, rode on her mother's hip. Maud put her down and she toddled after her brothers. At eight, Samuel was a year older than Gideon, and Peter, at six, was a year younger.

Maud didn't speak beyond a brisk greeting. Gideon watched as she prepared oatmeal while his cousins gathered on the benches.

Then Clare came in. This was Gideon's mother as he knew her best. Her brown hair was coiled up and fastened with pins. Her dress was cut to show her waist and her cheeks were like peach skin. She offered Uncle Thomas her hand and he stood as he took it. His posture changed. He drew his shoulders back and his unshaven face now looked vital and manly rather than sinister.

"Clare, help me with this, will you?" Maud asked suddenly. "Stir that pot for me."

Gideon didn't like the way Thomas smiled, but he didn't know why.

Samuel kneeled on the kitchen bench beside his brother and whispered in his ear. Both of them laughed. Thomas's look was thunder.

"Boys, show Gideon the cows," Maud suggested.

Gideon was taken into the yard for questioning.

"Have you got a slingshot?" Samuel asked and then without waiting for an answer, "I have, see?"

Before Gideon could answer, Samuel went on, "You can play with it later, if you like. Have you come to live here forever? Ma says charity begins at home."

"It's not charity." Gideon tried to sound confident. "It's our home too."

It was strange to use the word "home" for Ormesleep Farm, but he felt he needed to stake his claim.

"Our dad leathers you if you make too much noise

in the morning," Peter announced, feeling left out. He picked up a stick and smacked the water in the trough with it, sending drops into the air. They caught the light, a shower of diamonds dropping onto the dirt.

"Our dad's a farmer. What does yours do?"

"He's a private secretary."

"What does that mean?"

"He writes letters and reads books."

Samuel didn't seem to think much of this. "Our father has a herd of sheep and dogs. And a shotgun."

Gideon started to tell him about the library, but Samuel interrupted him. "Come and see our cows."

Gideon had never been in a barn before. The air was sweet with dusty hay. Things with hooks and claws and blades were hung on the wall. They stood looking up at them. Samuel named for Gideon's benefit: scythe, pitchfork, rake, and flail. They looked like instruments of torture, not farming implements.

"That's Daisy and this is Dolly." Peter pointed to the cows in the stall. They cropped at the hay with their flat teeth. They were delicate shades of brown smudged with cream.

"Can you milk a cow?"

"No"—Gideon felt wanting—"but I know Latin."

Samuel spat on the floor. "Book learning won't keep you warm or fed."

"It will too!"

Samuel hit Gideon. The sudden blow shocked him more than it hurt, making him slow to react. He lunged at Samuel, knocking him down. Gideon felt Peter's arms around his legs. Elbows slammed against rib cages and fingers pulled at hair. Boot heel scraped the skin from shins. No one would give in.

"Samuel! Peter! Come on, now." Maud's voice rang out. "Fetch Gideon."

They broke off. Samuel and Peter ran for the house, leaving Gideon to dust off the dirt and follow them in for breakfast.

On the Orme

"SON, LOOK."

Gideon stood beside his father. The sun made a fuss of setting, bleeding red and orange into the sea. Gideon could smell salt. The vastness of the ocean was still new to him.

"This is the Orme, Gideon."

Ahead of them the outcrop of land dipped to meet the waves below. Behind them was the track leading back to the farm, flanked by yellow gorse and purple heather.

"I don't like it here." Gideon blurted out the words. "I

mean the farm. And the village."

Bath was rows of graceful townhouses. Children played with hoops and skipping ropes in the lanes. There was the sound of laughter and street hawkers. The smell of chestnuts roasting in the glowing braziers. Rolling carriage wheels followed the horses' hooves that rang out on the cobbles. At dusk the oil lamps were lit, hanging in the misty streets like magic lanterns carried by giants.

Here in Ormeshadow, ragged children ran along in the muddy wheel-ruts of carts. They stared at strangers. When Gideon said hello, they continued to stare in silence. There was only a chapel and an inn. Unlike the cornfields around Bath, there was coarse grass fighting against the wind coming in off the sea.

"Gideon, this is my land so it's yours, too."

"All the farm?"

"No, this half. *This half,* mind. That's important. From over there"—he pointed back across the miles to where they'd come from—"to all the way over there, to the tip of the Orme."

"This is the Orme?"

"She's beneath your feet. Behind us, where the land rises before it dips, are her hindquarters. This ridge is her backbone."

Her spine ran away from them down the centre of the Orme. Limestone showed through in patches, seamed with lichen. She was taking shape beneath Gideon's feet.

Sheep scattered as they walked. Gideon felt they were high up enough to reach out and grasp the sky. The gulls that hovered and fell on the wind had stopped soaring and screaming, retiring to holes in the cliff faces around the bay. The air was changing from warm amber to a cool, dusky blue.

"This is my favourite place, Gideon."

"Not the library?"

Gideon meant the old master's library in Bath, where his father worked. Sometimes Gideon was allowed to go there with him and look at the rows of spines, gold lettering tooled into the leather. Rolled maps were stored in brass tubes. There were butterflies skewered in cases, beautiful things the size of a man's hand, their iridescent wings marked with blind eyes for protection. Gideon had wanted to know why they were so dangerous that, even in death, they had to be contained. His father had laughed.

Gideon wished he could take back the question about which place his father liked best because he looked sad.

"Where there are books there's learning. There's no finer thing, but a man needs more. The soul must be fed, not just stomach and mind. He needs peace. Some people find it in church. I've always found it here."

Gideon slid his hand into his father's.

"Your grandfather used to bring me here. He was

called James. He used to tell me stories about the Orme."

They reached the tip of the spine, where the gentle incline peaked, just behind the head. The Orme was a strip of land, dividing the bay in half, and was symmetrical on either side of the ridge. Off to the east there was an inlet where the river met the sea after its journey down the valley, where more sheltered, prosperous lives were led.

"Look at those." His father showed him the rocky outcrops on either side of the Orme. "Those are her ears."

"Do dragons have ears?"

"And noses. See?"

The dropping outcrop was her snout, bumps marking her nostrils. Gideon laughed.

"How long do we have to stay here?"

John gave him a sidelong look.

"There's no more work for me in Bath, or elsewhere. We're staying right here. Half the farm is ours. Never forget that and don't let anyone tell you otherwise. Your uncle Thomas is a fine farmer, but this place is too much for one man. I gave him a mighty chore when I left. I can only hope he'll forgive me."

They watched the sun slip away underwater.

"I knew I couldn't stay away, Gideon. Not forever."

The Slow-Blinking Eye

"GIDEON, WE HAVE TO go." John Belman broke the silence.

"No, I want to stay here. I want you to carry on telling me about the Orme."

"We don't seem to have much time together the way we used to. Samuel and Peter have never had what we do. Thomas is too hard on them." His father sounded like he was apologising. "Tell you what. Why don't we slip up here one evening in the week, just the two of us, and we can talk more?"

Gideon pulled a face, trying to delay his father, but they started to walk back to the farmhouse.

"A little longer, then, but not much. We shouldn't keep the others waiting."

Down at Ormesleep they would be laying the table for supper.

"Tell me some more about the dragon."

"What do you want to know?"

"Why did she come here?"

"The Orme was royalty among the dragons. Daughter of a king. Her father was fearsome and brave, but for a dragon he was also an original thinker. He planned harmony between dragons and men, who were always at war."

"An alliance between men and dragons?" Gideon was enraptured by the idea.

"Dragons live a long time and see great changes. Their king had foresight, knowing though small, men were cunning, and held the future in their hands."

"What did the king do?"

"He chose an ally among men."

Gideon could hear the storytelling in his father's voice.

"Who did the king choose?" Gideon was curious, and jealous. A king of men. Or a warrior.

"A shepherd."

"No!"

"Yes! Dragons can use their slow-blinking eyes to look into the heart of any man. The dragon king saw honesty and truth. Do you know what the man was called?"

Gideon shook his head. Something in his chest fluttered, trying to answer.

"Gideon Bellamans."

"Bellamans?"

"Yes, the origin of our name, Belman, is Bellamans. I called you Gideon for him. Gideon promised to be his emissary, carrying messages to the English thanes, for the sake of peace. No more arrows shot at the sky to kill dragons and no more villages burnt in revenge. It didn't please all men. Or dragons. There were some of his own kind who plotted against the king."

"Treason?"

"They attacked him during the great migration of dragons, when he'd be at his most tired from the flight."

"Did he fight back?" Gideon's eyes were wide with fear.

"Oh yes. He wasn't king for nothing. He battled for his life, as did his loyal followers. It must have been quite a sight, the last battle of the dragons."

Gideon could see them in shades of green and dark purple, in bronze and gold, wheeling around each other. This was no simple posturing. They were like kestrels, their huge talons leading their attack, slashing and clawing at each other. Fire streamed from their nostrils and their teeth were bared. There was a flurry of leathery wings as they grappled, trying to drag one another from the sky.

The sound. The sounds, louder than any other, shaking the earth and the sky. Screaming. Screeching. Howling. Such sounds, never to be heard again.

"What about the princess?" The Orme, a princess.

"She flew with her prince and her child, guarding her father's flanks with flame-dripping jaws. How she fought to protect her family. She was so fierce that several of their enemies had to work together to separate her from them."

"How did they do it?"

"They got between her and her calf."

Gideon imagined her, torn, trying to be everywhere at once until the mewing of her child overcame her. She broke away, her wings beating.

"What could she do, alone and surrounded? They taunted her, so many of them, dipping and diving around her until she was exhausted. Then they inflicted the most painful wound of all. They crushed her son between their great claws.

"The Orme's piercing cry cut through all the others, making those who had done the terrible deed back away, fearful and ashamed. She followed, her blind fury making her reckless. Finally, a blow knocked her from the sky and she fell to earth.

"The ground shook, again and again, as the bodies dropped from the heavens.

"The princess was left for dead, one body among many heaped upon the hills. Her leg was injured and all that came from her nostrils were sparks too small to ignite a flame.

"From where she lay, she could see the body of her father. He was on his side, panting. His chest was ripped open and his life leaked out. The Orme crawled over to him.

"'Go, daughter. Fly before they regroup and come back.'

"'No, I won't leave you.'

"'Yes, you will. I command you. Go and sleep and heal until our time comes again.'

"Before he died, her father told her his secret, of a man called Gideon Bellamans and where to find him."

Gideon could see the farmhouse now, smoke climbing from the chimney.

"The Orme was tired and weary because she had flown a long way after the battle. Tired and weary and heartsick. All her kin, all that she loved best in the world, gone. Her father. Her mate. Her child. She circled high in the sky, the circles becoming smaller and lower until she landed in the sea to cool herself and wash away the dirt and blood. She shifted her belly, the warmth of the sun finding her bones.

"When she sighed smoke curled from her nostrils. That was how Gideon Bellamans found her, weary and brokenhearted. To live such a long time and spend it feeling so low is a terrible thing."

Gideon tried to imagine such pain but couldn't. Instead he saw it all as his father described it, Gideon Bellamans's surprise as the beast turned her massive head to look at him. He stood on the cliff edge, unsure whether she was friend or foe, fixing him with her slow-blinking eyes. He didn't turn and run. She was the one trespassing, after all. He listened as she spoke and took in the crusts of blood along the deep gash on her leg.

"I will look after you," he announced, once he'd heard her story.

The Orme looked at this man who she could kill with a swish of her tail and saw what her father saw and finally understood the nature of men. That such a brief life could burn so brightly and be so noble and so devious surprised her. Her father had been wise indeed.

"I will sleep," she told him. "I must heal and dream and wait for my time to come again."

She tried to eat the dead sheep he'd brought her with delicacy, but she was ravenous. She tipped back her head and chomped them down, her jaws working.

"You'll be dead when that time comes," she told him, looking for the man's fear. Not fear of her, but of death itself. There was none. He stood tall and nodded as though his own mortality were nothing to fear, being the natural order of things. "And so will your sons, as their sons will be and so on and so on." Then, with sadness, "You and I will not speak again, Gideon Bellamans."

"Then I will keep you safe and tell my sons to tell their sons, and their sons' sons and so on, that here lies a dragon and the Bellamanses must always shelter her and be there for her when she wakes from dreaming."

Closer to the farmhouse and Gideon could see Samuel's anxious face, peering from the window in search of them.

The Race

GIDEON MARVELLED HOW WHEN Thomas called Sweetheart to heel she came without question, just for the joy of being in his shadow.

"He'll never love anyone as much as he loves that dog," Maud had once complained out of her husband's earshot, banging pots about on the stove.

Nancy, Sweetheart's sister, made to follow, but Thomas held her back with a low, growling whistle. Sweetheart turned her longing eyes on him, grateful to be chosen, her pink tongue lolling.

Now Thomas, with only his two dogs, had brought the whole flock down to the shallow crossing place in the river to be washed.

The rest of the Belman men waited, in position.

"Your father has a God-given talent," John said to his nephew. "I've never seen a man with a talent for dogs like he has."

Samuel stood shivering in his shirtsleeves, waiting for the sun to warm him through. "I suppose so."

"No supposing at all, boy." Gideon had never heard his father call anyone *boy* before. "When he was your age he was training his first dog, all by himself. No one taught him how to. By the time he was fourteen, men were coming to him and asking him to pick them out a pup from the litter he'd bred and name his own price for it."

Samuel, stung, stared up the hill at his father.

"So why doesn't anyone come up here for pups any-more?" Gideon asked.

"Your grandfather put a stop to it all when Lord Jessop came all the way from Carrside in his carriage, offering Thomas a place, breeding and training his hounds for hunting. He had some funny notions about what was important, our father did, especially after our ma died. He didn't want us both leaving the farm. He did Thomas a disservice. Every man has a talent."

The sheep poured down on them as if a dam had broken and let them through. Thomas was whistling; shrill notes, low hoots and growls, a whole language only his girls understood. Gideon felt the same respect for him at that moment as he had when he watched the blacksmith shoeing a horse or his mother's needle fly across a piece of silk.

Thomas waved and John was in the water, wading in up to his thighs. The river swirled around him. The dogs guided the flock toward the gap in the bank. The boys stood with legs spread and arms out, helping the dogs to keep them from breaking away.

There was a crush of bleating sheep as they hovered at the river's edge. John grabbed the foremost sheep, one hand on the scruff of its neck and the other one deep in the fleece of its back, and heaved it into the river.

The alarmed sheep kicked until it landed in the water with a splash. The others followed, a woolly tributary, plunging into the water and coming out indignant and wet. They filled the field on the other side, this baptism not to cleanse their souls but their fleeces, ready for shearing as soon as they were dry.

Peter picked up the shearing shears, the blades hinged at one end. "You can carve them into pieces if you're not careful."

"Get off." Thomas took them off him. "They're not a toy."

Gideon sat on the wall, the cold seeping from the stone and into the seat of his trousers. Peter wandered away, punching Samuel as he went. Samuel hit him back, felling his brother with ease. They went at it in silence and their father left them to it.

"Come here."

Gideon jumped down but lingered by the wall.

"I said come here."

Overcome by the desire to run away, his legs refused to carry him to Thomas as instructed.

"I won't bite you." Thomas raised an eyebrow at him, gesture and words that were like Gideon's father's. Gideon obeyed.

"Here. Take them." Thomas offered him the shears.

Gideon took them, his fingers and thumb finding their rightful places. The oiled hinge offered little resistance and the shears responded with a dangerous snipping sound.

"You're a natural. We'll make a farmer of you yet." There was no pride or encouragement in his voice, just cold observation. "Careful, though. They can be lethal. You can take off teats and testicles along with the fleece. Not to mention fingertips."

The words "teat" and "testicle" sounded sore in themselves, making Gideon want to protect every fleshy part of himself.

"Peter's right. I've seen bad shearers take off skin and flesh from cutting too deep."

It was the most Gideon had ever heard his uncle say to anyone. That it was directed at him made Gideon feel it was an examination he had to pass. He wanted to rise to it and ask a question or make a clever comment that would make him worthy of his uncle's attention. Instead of the free banter he enjoyed with his father, he froze, unable to think of what to say.

Clare and Maud had joined them, leading the donkey and cart for taking the fleeces away. John strolled over and picked up the second pair of shears.

"What are you doing?" Clare asked.

"I'm the son of a sheep farmer." He shook his head at

their incredulous faces. "What did you think I was going to do today?"

Clare looked at him like he'd been concealing things from her.

"Let's see if you still have the knack or whether all those books have ruined you." Thomas gave his brother a rare smile. It looked odd on his narrow face.

The sheep had been penned with a run at one end of their enclosure. At the start and end of the run were trapdoors that could be lifted when one of the boys pulled on a rope. Samuel manned the first door and Gideon the second, while Peter stood on one of the fences making up the run and flicked the sheep with a switch to keep them moving. Once released by Gideon, the lone sheep was met by one of the men, brandishing blades.

"You go first, John. It's only fair to give you a head start."

John caught the ram and heaved it onto its hindquarters. Using a bale for balance, he tipped the sheep back at an angle. It realised the futility of its struggle and gave in. John's knees were wedged into the animal's fleshy belly rather than its ribs, to cause it the minimum of discomfort. One hand held the shears and the other gripped one of the forelegs.

Another sheep came out of the run to be caught by Thomas.

Gideon watched his father at the unfamiliar task. It was strange to see, as it was clearly once a well-practised chore. As he worked, John's fingers seemed to remember their disused skill. They found their way, pulling the wool back to bare it for the blades. He went from tummy to throat, from neck to flank, rolling the sheep from one side to the other until he reached the tail.

The fleece fell from the sheep in a single piece. It was worth more whole.

Thomas finished his a fraction sooner. Both men swapped from shears to clippers to trim the sheeps' hooves, and they were set free at the same time. Without their coats they were scrawny, naked creatures. They ran into the far corner of the field in shame.

Maud went to take Thomas's fleece, telling Clare to fetch John's. Maud taught her how to cut off the dunged wool and twist and roll the fleece into a neat bundle. She was about to fling them on the cart, but Thomas shouted to her as he struggled to get to grips with the next ewe. He told the women to make them into separate piles, one his and the other for John's fleeces. They would count them at the end.

"But—" Maud began.

"Leave it, woman."

Maud shrugged and dropped the fleece. Gideon saw his mother look to his father, who nodded. She left his bundled fleece where it lay.

While they sheared the second pair, Gideon ran over to touch the fleece. The wool was coarse and greasy. He sniffed his hand where he'd touched it, pulling a face.

Maud cocked her head on one side. "It's not very nice, is it? It's the grease they make. It keeps them snug and dry. Feel the other side."

By contrast it was soft and luxurious, like thick felt. He put his cheek to it and his aunt did the same, giggling.

"Gideon! You idiot. Get back here."

It was Samuel. Gideon was surprised that another sheep was in the run, the men nearly having finished with the second set of sheep.

With each animal, his father's movements became defter, his fingers faster, although he remained a fleece behind his brother. They paused only to take swigs from their water flasks, not daring to stop for longer.

It was furious work. The sun passed its highest point, but they pressed on until early afternoon, neither calling it time to eat until Maud demanded they stop. By then, they'd shed their shirts, grime and grease on their chests and arms, under their fingernails and in their hair.

Thomas took his bread from Clare.

"You smell of sheep," she announced.

"That's the smell of good, honest work, in case you didn't recognise it."

He made to lunge at her and she darted away, stifling a squeal. She seemed in good humour for once. Peter counted the fleeces and declared them neck and neck so far. John had caught up with Thomas.

The afternoon was harder. Stopping to rest gave their overworked muscles time to complain. Their wrists and backs ached, but both men were at pains not to seem bothered. They took up their positions and the sheep were stripped of their bounty.

Gideon watched his mother's face glow as she willed the men on, her eyes darting from one to the other. Through the whole day she'd stayed that way, ignoring Charity's pleas to come for a walk with her and Maud. Clare brushed off the small hands clutching at her skirt, annoyed at the distraction.

"You, pay attention." Gideon, too busy looking at his mother, had not lifted his gate, delaying the next sheep, which was for Thomas. His cheeks burned, shamed by his cousins' angry looks that suggested he'd tried to cheat to help his father get ahead.

The mood of the day was souring. It was finally spoilt when Thomas came apart at the clipping of a set of hooves. Blood jetted out, high arcs landing some distance away in the grass in a crimson stain. In his haste he had clipped too close and caught an artery.

"Damn." Thomas could see his lead slipping away.

John had finished his sheep and dropped it. It ran away bleating.

"Hold him still."

Thomas bridled, despite the sense in John's order. The animal could bleed to death.

John motioned to Maud, who pulled the string and knife from her apron pocket, which she carried for just this purpose. He knelt before the bleeding sheep, hot blood splashing him. He bound the ankle to stem the flow to the wound. The blood slowed to a dribble and then stopped.

"Clare, get that rope and tie her up on the cart. I'll need you to cut the string off when I tell you to."

He rinsed the blood off himself with the rest of his drinking water.

"It was just bad luck, Thomas. It could have happened to either of us. Do you remember the year that I did exactly the same on three sheep in a row?"

"We've not finished yet." Thomas's face was set hard, and nothing John could say would soften it. "Pick up your shears."

So, they began again, this time with John at an advantage. Despite this, his hands dithered, where before they'd been certain. Gideon watched his father's every move, convinced he was slowing down deliberately, just enough to let Uncle Thomas win by a believable margin. A skill in itself.

Clare snorted, saying nothing. Maud patted John's back. "Hard luck but well done, brother. How many years has it been since you've done this?"

Thomas shot her a furious look and she bit her lip. He called his girls to him and walked away, carrying his shirt in one hand so it trailed on the ground. Nancy and Sweetheart loped along beside him.

He'd left the rest of the family there to load the cart. John lifted Charity onto the fleeces, laying her sleepy head on the cushion of warm wool. Peter and Samuel pulled the donkey's harness to keep it moving while Clare and Maud walked up ahead, side by side but silent and separate.

"You let him win." Gideon tried not to sound like an accuser. Fatigue had gathered in the creases around his father's eyes.

"Sometimes it takes a better man to lose than to win."

"But you were equal," protested Gideon.

"For Thomas to win, Gideon, I must always lose."

Lessons

GIDEON SAT AT THE kitchen table with his cousins and father, a book open before them at the final chapter.

Samuel struggled with his letters more than Peter and much more than Gideon, who was better than either of them. Gideon kept silent, even though he wanted to jump in and shout out the words that ran across the page, fleeing from Samuel's forefinger as he attempted to follow them.

Thomas came in, banging the door behind him.

"Carry on, Samuel," John prompted, "we want to know how it ends. You're the man to tell us."

"You're filling their heads with nonsense." Thomas put an end to Samuel's reading.

Thomas had stripped to the waist to wash at the pump outside. Water dripped from his hair where he'd dunked his head in the stream of water. Sparkling drops fell onto his chest. Primal and predatory, he paced about the kitchen like it was a cage. His nakedness made Gideon uncomfortable. His father was always properly clothed.

Gideon looked away but he could still hear the sound of the rough towel rubbing skin.

"A man should be able to read and write more than his own name."

"Meaning he's an idiot if he can't," Thomas retorted.

"I didn't say that. There's fools who can read and there's clever men who can't. And I know you read and write as well as I do when you want to."

"For all it helped you, professor."

Gideon's mother stood in the doorway. Gideon thought Uncle Thomas's bare chest must make her feel uncomfortable too because her eyes flitted over him in an unfocused way too. Breathy and girlish, she looked ravishing in her best green dress.

"Mr. Thomas Belman," she announced, "may I present your wife, Mrs. Maud Alice Belman."

Maud's boot heel struck each step on the stairs. Her mass of hair had been tamed. Clare had brushed it a hundred times until it shone and then fixed it into an intricate knot at the nape of her neck. Clare had made Maud a new dress in the same fabric as her own.

Charity cried at the stranger in their midst, so Gideon pulled her onto his lap so as not to spoil his aunt's special moment. Samuel and Peter were openmouthed.

Maud curtsied. Clare slipped an arm around her waist. "Isn't she a stunner?" They stood side by side and Maud suffered by comparison. The red flush of excitement on her neck and chest was highlighted by the green wool. The shape of the dress could not be faulted, but the shade was misjudged. It made ashes of her complexion and bleached the colour from her eyes.

Thomas did not pause from moving the towel across his chest. "A fine piece of craftsmanship. Pity it's so wasted."

Aunt Maud's boots clattered on the stairs as she fled

upstairs. Gideon's mother followed.

Gideon never saw his aunt wear the dress again.

~

There was silence in the schoolroom after the master caned the new boy, Timothy, for the crime of being left-handed. Orphaned Timothy had come to live with his aunt in the village. Gideon was glad to hand over the mantle of newcomer, even though he'd been at the school for several years now.

The schoolmaster, Mr. Taylor, sat at the front of the classroom. On his desk were his inkwell, his writing papers, and the class register. The register was a ledger of attendance, in which the children were reduced to a list of names and columns of ticks. Mr. Taylor wrote down the reason for their absence, such as *scarlatina* or *kept home for harvesting*. Gideon was so close that he could hear the master's pen nib scratching the paper as he wrote his important letters. Chalk dust still clung to his black frock coat. The sated cane rested on the window ledge. The man took out his pocket watch and checked the time. He waited for the hand to move a fraction and then snapped it shut and put it away.

"Jenny," he called out, "the bell."

Everyone knew the girls were Mr. Taylor's favourites.

Jenny stood before the master's desk in her blue pinafore, heaving the heavy brass hand bell up and down to mark the end of the school day. The clapper struck the sides, making a peal too loud for the small room.

"Eliza Dorcus"—another girl stood to attention when the master called her name—"you may stay behind and clean the blackboard."

Gideon glanced over to Eliza. Her hands rolled into a single fist, which she held low over her belly, unhappy to be the recipient of such favours. She was one of the Ormeshadow children mocked by the valley pupils as a straggly gang, many of whom were shoeless and lice-ridden. Sometimes Gideon looked back along the cool green corridors of trees to see Eliza Dorcus in the distance, hurrying to catch up. Late Eliza was her nickname. Her mother, Hettie, was widowed and needed her oldest daughter to help her manage all her other children. She'd be expected home, and Gideon could see her fretting that Mr. Taylor would make her late.

There was the sound of heavy boots at the back of the room, too heavy to be a child's. They all turned to see John Belman.

Samuel nudged Gideon. He shrugged in reply to the quizzical look from his cousin. When Samuel and Peter sat at the table at night, telling their uncle about the day's lessons, John would nod and listen, but there would be a shadow of a frown on his face at the errors they recited. Afterward he'd ask Gideon if they had misunderstood or whether that was how the lesson had been taught. Caught between truth and lies, Gideon didn't want to answer. His father could tell the truth of the matter and didn't press him to reply. What if his father had come here to tell the schoolmaster about all his mistakes? Gideon had seen his best suit laid out on the bed that morning. Had he thought of wearing it and changed his mind?

"Eliza, you may go. I will see to the board later."

"Thank you, sir." Eliza pushed her way through the throng of children crowding to the door. She darted out as though she might be pulled back at any moment.

"John, what a pleasure. Come in."

Mr. Taylor rose, his gold watch fob shining from his waistcoat. John Belman was in his work shirt and braces, cap in hand. The two men shook hands like old friends who were delighted to see each other again. Samuel lingered by the door, wanting to be involved.

"What are you waiting for?" The master turned on him, licking his fleshy lips. Samuel ran outside to join his brother. Gideon made to follow, but his father kept him there with a hand on his shoulder.

"Mr. Taylor and I went to this school together. I'm sorry I've not come to say hello earlier."

Gideon felt a stuttering anxiety in his stomach. He wasn't sure why his father had held him back or what was expected of him.

"We both sat at the front together, there." John pointed to their desks.

The master was seated again, while John remained standing before the desk, like a reprimanded student. Gideon realised his father was nervous. He had released his grip on Gideon's shoulder and was running his cap through his hands. Hands that were once soft and spotless, wearing kid gloves to handle rare volumes, now coarse from ploughing and planting. Dirt was ingrained in the patterns on his fingertips.

"Are you well, John?"

"Very well. What of you? Is there a Mrs. Taylor?"

"No, I'm unmarried, but then, all these children are mine." He waved a hand at the empty classroom. "What about your brother, Thomas?"

The schoolmaster's lips were thin as he said it. Gideon had heard the stories of how Uncle Thomas had caught the schoolmaster alone as often as he could, taunting him until he cried. His father used to intervene, chasing his brother off, and looked away while Richard dried his tears.

"Thomas is well enough."

"His daughter will be joining us soon, won't she? I look forward to it."

Gideon could not imagine how Charity would manage in class. She was already the worst of her parents: Thomas's temper and Maud's timidity.

The schoolmaster seemed to be waiting for something.

"Mr. Taylor was clever, and he worked very hard," John said after a pause. "If you work hard to apply yourself as he did, you might just become a schoolmaster like him, Gideon."

"Not at all." Mr. Taylor seemed embarrassed and pleased all at once. "None of us were as clever as your father."

There was silence.

"I thought you had great ambitions for yourself, John. Expectations of your achievements were high when you went off to university."

"I met my wife, Clare. I was suddenly a man with a family who had to earn a living."

"Oh, I see." The schoolmaster was solemn, but his eyes danced.

~

Father and son walked home under malingering clouds, picking blackberries from the hedgerows. At this time of year Maud sent the children out with cloth sacks to harvest what was ripe, be it berries or hazelnuts or fat, leathery mushrooms. Gideon liked to watch her making jams and pies, her hands deft as she worked the dough. When she washed the fruit, spiders climbed from the basin to flee the flood.

The blackberries were pale red, moving through to black and purple as they ripened in the autumn sunshine. They grew in luscious clusters, the ready ones falling into their hands without resistance. Nettles stung Gideon's hands as he foraged, leaving white welts in red patches on his skin. The prize was worth the pain, though. The fruits burst in his mouth, sometimes tart, sometimes sweet.

Gideon thought about what his father had said about being a man with a family and having to earn a living. Once he had taken Gideon to see the university. It was a sacred place of high arches carved in white stone, and through the hallowed halls walked men of learning with books under their arms, their minds on lofty things. Their discussions were of Greek philosophy, not the price of wool.

John Belman had glowed as he stood there, but afterward said to his son, "I have done nothing, Gideon. I am nothing. Those men are truly great. Their dedication to learning is unwavering. They thirst for knowledge the way I thirsted for your mother. She is very beautiful."

To think of it made Gideon's chest hurt. *I am nothing*.

He turned to his father. "Why did you leave the university?"

"Leave it. It's long past."

"Was it because of us?"

"I said it's long past."

Gideon understood then that there were things they kept from each other. Things Gideon couldn't tell his father and things his father could never tell him.

Sweetheart

"SETTLE DOWN, GIRL."

Thomas perched on an upturned barrel in the yard. Sweetheart sat between his knees looking out at the world as he stroked her, his tone soothing. Without his normal gruffness, his voice was as rich and deep as his brother's, with the same lilt.

It looked like he was just making a fuss of her, but Gideon knew better. His uncle was searching for something, his hands moving over her coat. He lingered around her neck and ears with all the care of a physician and once satisfied, he checked her belly and hindquarters. Then he went back to her head and took her snout, prising open her jaws to look in her mouth.

His eyebrows furrowed.

Sweetheart lifted a paw and laid it on his forearm as if

asking for something. She glanced at him and then away, showing him the whites of her eyes. Thomas inspected each of her paws in turn, each claw and each of the fleshy pink pads.

"What do you want?"

Thomas seemed so engrossed that when he spoke it startled Gideon.

"Aunt Maud sent me to find you. Supper's nearly ready." Gideon came closer. "Is she sick?"

"Something's bothering her." Thomas carried on his examination. "But I don't know what."

Sweetheart had started to do strange things for a herder. She'd been nipping at the sheep's heels to keep them in line, the frightened herd scattering before her, bleating in alarm. When Thomas scolded her she slunk toward him, full of remorse.

Even though the dogs cared for no one but Thomas, Gideon loved to watch them at work. They were never idle. When they weren't in the field they'd herd chickens and children around the yard, just for the ecstasy of having a purpose.

"Can you fix her?"

Gideon's anxiety over her affected Thomas, softening his reply.

"I don't know. That depends on what's wrong. I'll keep watching her for now."

"Shall I fetch her some water or meat?"

"No, she's had plenty."

Thomas patted Sweetheart's rump and got up. She trotted after him, but he ordered her to her bed in the barn. As they walked to the kitchen, Thomas put a hand on Gideon's shoulder. It was a short-lived affection. As Clare opened the door before them, Thomas's hand fell away and hung by his side like dead wood.

~

The sheep were in a panic. They had scattered to the far corners of the field, deserting their dead compatriot. The ewe lay on her side, her fleece a matted mess of dried blood. One ear and cheek had been torn off in the struggle, revealing muscle and gleaming bone beneath.

"Don't do that."

Samuel was prodding the eviscerated animal with a stick. Its uncoiled intestines were exposed, pink tubes lying in the grass.

"I said don't, Samuel."

Samuel looked back at John and then dropped the stick amid the innards. Gideon turned away. Thomas was gazing at the carcass, his arms folded. Gideon's father, by contrast, couldn't keep still. He kept searching Thomas's face, which remained impassive.

"It could have been a stray dog," John said.

The sheep stared at them, accusation in its fixed eyes.

"It was Sweetheart," Thomas replied.

"You can't be sure."

"Why do you think she's run off?"

Nancy sat by Thomas's legs, her presence giving her impunity, but Sweetheart was nowhere to be seen.

A crow landed nearby and paraded around the corpse. The bird's liquid black eyes were shiny and dead looking. When Gideon shooed it away it squawked at him and flapped its angry wings.

"I need to find her," Thomas announced. "Get rid of that sheep. Bury it or something."

"Thomas, let me help you."

"I don't need your help. She's just a dog." Thomas turned away from John.

"Don't be like that. You know what I mean. You don't have to do this on your own."

Thomas picked up his pace, leaving them behind.

"What will you do?" John called after him. "Thomas, what will you do?"

~

The pail clinked as Gideon shut the barn door. It was his turn to do the milking. There was the rotten, sweet smell of the hay. The docile cows in their stalls sniffed at it with their delicate pink noses.

A noise from the corner startled Gideon. Thomas sat cross-legged on the floor, his dog in his lap. Sweetheart shivered and shook. As Gideon came closer, treading slowly so not to startle them, he could see it was more than a fever. Sweetheart's eyes were glassy in her seizure. Her rigid legs jerked. She had wet herself, the urine staining Thomas's trousers in dark, irregular patches.

Knowing the severity of her crime, Sweetheart had stayed away all day, finally coming home to Ormesleep, where Thomas had found her as she hid in the barn. Telltale blood caked the fur of her muzzle. The sight made Gideon's heart lurch in his chest.

Sweetheart stopped fitting and lay there panting. "I'm here now. I'll look after you," Thomas crooned, putting his head against hers. At the sound of his voice, her tail thumped the ground.

The long barrel of the shotgun glinted from where it was propped against the wall. The oiled dark metal waited patiently, knowing it wouldn't be long. Thomas rocked back and to in a motion normally reserved for calming fractious infants.

"Is she all right?" Gideon took a few more steps.

Thomas looked up, his unguarded face contorted. The tears gathering in his eyes now spilled down his cheeks.

Sweetheart tried to lick them away. "Go away."

"Shall I get my dad?"

"No! Just go away!" Sweetheart became fretful at the sound of her master shouting so Thomas lowered his voice. "Get out."

"You don't have to do this on your own." His father's words came out. His father would know how to help. And Gideon wanted to help Sweetheart. He wanted to help Thomas.

"She's mine. This is my business." Thomas looked at Gideon as though he'd put a knife in him. "Stop looking at me."

Gideon put out a hand.

"Stop looking at me." Thomas's lip curled into a lupine snarl, threatening to bite if Gideon came too close.

Gideon ran outside. The abandoned pail clattered on the cobbles. He knew his father would have wanted him to fetch him, but it didn't seem right to. He had already intruded. He dithered in the yard. There was a ring around the moon to warm it, in shades of green and red. It would be a cold night.

The gunshot rang out. It was so loud that it filled the yard, and then the fields around Ormesleep Farm and then all of Ormeshadow itself. Gideon was surprised it took so long for the rest of the Belmans to come running from the house.

Treasure in Her Belly

IT WAS AUTUMN, BUT up on the Orme there were the last vestiges of summer in the warmth that lingered on the breeze. Down in the valley the leaves were already the colour of claret. Gideon loved autumn. It was the time of year that he filled his pockets with treasures. Rich conkers, smooth once prised from their spiky shells. Acorns in their cups. Then suddenly, the trees were bonfires. The blaze of reds and yellows burnt the boughs to stark blackness.

Here in Ormeshadow, autumn meant toil. A shoring up against winter. Stubble smoked from the harvested fields and wood was stacked under cover to season. There was foraging for nuts and berries. In every kitchen things were smoked or pickled and packed in stone jars.

Knowing the winter months would mean more time confined to the farm, Gideon and his father came up to the Orme as often as they could.

"Dad, where did the chair come from?"

"What, son?"

"The one in the kitchen, with the carvings on it."

Gideon studied the chair whenever he was alone, which wasn't often as the kitchen was the hub of the house. His fingers traced out the patterns on the back.

Dragons and skeletons entwined with crowns, necklaces, lances, and swords. There were coins marked with long dead faces and rings set with gems. A hoard of treasure. The arms and legs were dragons, pockmarked with holes from greedy woodworms. Regal and dilapidated, the chair sat at the head of the Belman table.

Once his father sat in it at supper. Uncle Thomas took a seat on the far end of one of the benches, simmering just below the point of eruption, as though some unpardonable breach of etiquette had occurred.

"You mean the dragon chair." There was no other chair in the house, only benches and stools. "It's been in the family for generations."

"It's very fancy."

"Once a man offered my grandfather his finest thoroughbred horse for it, but he wouldn't have it."

"Is it worth that much?"

"Something's only worth what a man is willing to pay for it."

"Why didn't he sell it?"

"It's a family heirloom." His father's pause added drama. "And it's a treasure map of the Orme."

Gideon rolled his eyes and play punched him in the ribs. They fought until they were laughing so hard that Gideon got a stitch.

"I'm serious."

"About what?" Gideon wiped his eyes.

"It's a map. The carvings reveal where the treasure is. If only I knew how to read it."

Gideon laughed again.

"If you don't believe me, ask your uncle Thomas. There's not a Belman man or woman who doesn't know the tale."

"Except me. And Mother."

John stopped smiling and put his hands in his pockets. "I meant to tell you all the Orme stories, but I wasn't sure if we'd ever come back here."

Gideon wanted to bite his own tongue off. With a few words he'd made his father sad. He tried to rally him.

"What would a dragon want with treasure?"

"Dragons are like magpies. They like sparkling, glittering things. Things fashioned from the bounty of the earth, gems and metals from deep in the ground. Some people used to think gold attracts dragons, but I don't know if it isn't dragons that attract gold."

"Who made the chair?"

"Jonah Belman. He was your great-great-great-grandfather."

Gideon whistled as he tried to imagine someone so old.

"Jonah wasn't much of a sheep farmer, but he had a talent. He knew wood." John snorted. "Jonah's carving.

Thomas and his dogs. Me and my book learning. Your mother, the seamstress. All that skill languishing in Ormeshadow. Anyway, Jonah was a dreamer who could spend hours whittling at wood, looking for the shapes in it. So when an afternoon went by and he hadn't come home no one was surprised. But when night fell his wife got worried. As dreamy as he was, his stomach normally brought him back to the real world.

"In the end Jonah was gone for three whole weeks. His family thought he'd been swallowed by the sea. They found him wandering on the Orme, raving. His arm was broken. His clothes were in tatters and he'd grown a beard."

"Where'd he been?"

"No one ever found out. He said he fell down a hole and landed in the belly of the Orme. And he was thin because down in the dark all there was to eat were tiny blind fish that lived in rock pools. He could tell how far he'd fallen from a single shaft of light streaming into the darkness. He was lucky he didn't snap his neck when he landed."

John Belman spoke as if he'd heard the story from Jonah himself.

"What's that got to do with treasure?"

"Seawater and treasure were what he found there."

"In her belly?"

"Dragons have as many bellies as cows, and not all for food."

"That's silly."

"No! Listen! There's gold under the Orme. Jonah carved it all into a chair."

Gideon thought of the sceptre and the crown.

"So why didn't he go back and get it?"

"He didn't want it. He said if anyone else did they'd have to work it out for themselves from the chair. He was a delicate soul by all accounts. People said a stint underground sent him mad." John looked at him sideways. "Do you hold such baubles and trinkets to be the most valuable things in the world?"

Gideon considered the question.

"No, not to have riches for themselves, but I care for what you can do with them."

"And what would you do with a fortune?"

"I'd buy us a house of our own in Bath, with a library full of books stacked from floor to ceiling. There'd be a wardrobe full of pretty dresses to make Mother happy."

His father laughed. "What about you? What would you want for yourself?"

Gideon nearly replied, *My own room with a big bed in it and a window* but thought better of it.

"I'd learn everything there is to know and give lectures at the assembly rooms for everyone who wants to listen."

His father used to take him to the assembly rooms in Bath. He didn't understand all of the lectures, but he watched the upturned, eager faces of the audience and their animated conversations afterward.

"Dad, what was important to Jonah, then, if he didn't care for gold?"

"Gideon, I think when a man has spent three weeks down in a hole with no food, no warmth, and no hope of rescue, surrounded by a king's ransom, he comes to understand the true value of things."

They walked on, Gideon considering the lesson in this.

An Argument

GIDEON WOKE UP IN the dark. For a moment he wasn't sure where he was, even though he'd slept in the closet for years.

Once, soon after their arrival, Maud made Charity sleep in the closet and put Gideon in the bed upstairs with the boys. The girl had screamed loud enough to wake the dead as soon as the door was shut on her. Maud left her there, angry because Charity never minded anything she was told.

That night Samuel had stayed awake, kicking Gideon

as soon as he drifted off into dreaming. When Gideon finally kicked him back, Samuel ran from the room and told his uncle. John Belman came in and sat at Gideon's feet, admonishing him for his ingratitude when his cousins had been so welcoming toward him. He was disappointed. Very disappointed.

Samuel swung on the bedpost as Gideon received his telling off. Charity's screeching continued from below and everyone was secretly glad when Thomas came home and bellowed at Charity that if she didn't stop crying he would give her something to cry about.

The next night Charity had her own bed, as narrow as a plank, in the attic, and Gideon was glad to return to the privacy of his closet.

Lying in the dark, Gideon could hear someone moving about in the kitchen. He got up and peeped through the gap in the door panels, expecting Thomas. The figure lit a lamp and put it down before him on the table. In the smoking yellow light, Gideon could see it was his father.

John Belman took off his coat and sat in the dragon chair. Gideon opened the door a fraction, ready to go to him, despite the late hour, but another voice stopped him.

"John?"

It was his mother, her voice full of unfamiliar timidity. "John, is that you?"

"Yes."

He didn't turn to her. Gideon wasn't used to this indifference. Whenever John Belman came into a room, he always sought out his wife's face first.

"John, it's late. Come to bed."

His father snorted.

"Come to bed, love. Please. We can talk there. We'll wake Gideon if we stay here."

"I'm forever at your bidding, aren't I?" Such unaccustomed sharpness.

Gideon waited for the flash of anger that was his mother through and through. Instead she was meek when she put out the candle she carried and sat beside her husband.

"I was frightened. You went off in such a state." She still looked frightened, even though he was back.

"Where's Thomas?" John asked.

"He went out soon after you."

"Is Maud back?"

"No. Not yet." Maud had been gone for a full day, helping Mother Wainwright to deliver Hettie Dorcus's baby.

"Were you glad to see her out of the way?"

"It wasn't like that!" Clare hissed, showing some of her mettle. "It wasn't planned!"

"Don't you dare speak to me in that tone. Don't you dare so much as look at me the wrong way ever again!"

John Belman was furious. He leant over, the back of his hand raised. Clare sat, transfixed, not making a sound. Gideon's cry stuck in his throat and he thought it would choke him.

"Go on, do it, then, if it'll make you feel better." The look on Clare's face suggested that making him feel better was the last thing on her mind. They waited for the blow to fall. John's hand hovered, already losing momentum.

"Clare, I'm sorry, I'm sorry . . ." John reached for her. "I don't know what came over me."

She flinched even though the danger had passed. His face hardened.

"It would suit you well, wouldn't it? For me to be the villain. In all these years I've never put an angry hand on you."

"No, John. It's my fault. It's always my fault, isn't it?"

"What do you mean by that?"

"Oh, you know."

"No, tell me."

"You still blame me for us having to leave Bath. You miss your pens and papers and precious library."

"When have I ever blamed you?"

"No, you never said it aloud. But you didn't blame your precious Lord Bellingham, either, did you?"

"I resigned, didn't I? It was the greatest protest I could make."

"If I'd been you and a man embarrassed my wife that way I would have taken him outside and bloodied his face!" Clare's whispering was loud and angry.

"Clare, he was a muddled, lonely old man. Sometimes he got confused. What he said was improper, yes, but he never touched you, did he? He never harmed you."

"Harm? Harm?" They were locked together, struggling over their discordant truths. "No harm that you were left without references and no work to go to. No harm when my reputation was questioned when it was him who told me to sit on his knee in front of all those fine people. No harm when we had to leave our home."

"We have a roof over our heads and a living."

"Yes, scraping in the dirt."

"So this is why you did it, Clare? To punish me?"

What had she done that was so terrible? Gideon tried to think what it might have been, but there was nothing.

Meanwhile, John and Clare were no further on. The argument was circling back to the start.

"I love you," he said.

"You say you love me. I hear the words, but I don't feel them. How can I not feel them?"

"I don't know. I tell you every day. I don't know what other people mean when they say I love you, but I know what I mean and it's the same every time I say it. It means *I will be loyal, I will be faithful, I will be gentle, and I will be kind.*"

Clare shrugged, unimpressed by kindness.

"Teach me, then. Teach me what it is you want."

"I can't. It's either in you or it isn't."

"And it's in Thomas?" His voice was flint.

"No." She sounded confused. "Yes."

"Then it's in me, too." They were oblivious to everything now. The world had been reduced to only the two of them in a circle of lamplight.

"No, it's not. You're saying what you think I want to hear."

"Clare, I don't understand you. What do you want?"

"I want the sort of love that can't be cured." The words bubbled up. "The sort of love you'd kill for. Die for."

The dragon chair screeched as John jumped up. He seized her shoulders, forcing her to her feet. She was a rag doll in his hands.

"Isn't it better to have the sort of love that you live for?"

Her mouth was sullen, like Charity's when she'd been thwarted.

"If I died for you, would that prove how much I love you? Would it?" John didn't release her.

She didn't answer him. Nothing was right. Nothing he said. Nothing he could do. Gideon wanted to shout. To make her listen. To break her stubborn silence. He knew he wouldn't. He knew he shouldn't trespass.

John let her go and she dropped back onto the bench.

"Go back to bed," he told her. He put on his coat.

"Where are you going?"

"Never you mind."

"You won't go looking for Thomas, will you?"

"No." John's voice was like a knife's edge. It was a mistake to say his brother's name.

"When will you come back?"

"I said go to bed."

Clare obeyed. John blew out the lamp. He sat like a king stripped of everything but his throne, which was only a fancy wooden chair carved with imagined beasts. John cried.

Gideon hesitated. He'd never seen his father cry before and it frightened him. He wanted him to stop. He was fused to the floor by the cold that numbed his feet. It kept him there as his father left, quietly closing the farmhouse door behind him.

Gideon ran to the door when he could finally move, suddenly more afraid of his father's absence than his tears. "Dad?"

It was too late. His father had gone and the wind blew the words back in his face. It was too late to get dressed and run after him.

Something glinted from the kitchen table, shown up in the moonlight. It was a pledge in gold. An oath made of metal. Gideon held his father's wedding ring. He stood outside his mother's door for a long time, thinking about what to do for the best, and then went back to his closet and closed the door.

Death on the Orme

"GIDEON, GO OUTSIDE."

"But—"

"Do as I tell you." His mother's knuckles were white as she gripped the arm of the dragon chair. "Do it now."

"You'd better go too," Maud addressed Samuel and Peter, "and take Charity with you."

The kitchen was reduced by the number of the men who had crowded in. They shuffled to the edges of the room to make way for the children who filed past them. These strangers had come, bearing the body. They'd swaddled the dead man in a clean sheet.

The fishermen were accustomed to death, it being one of their many bounties from the sea. Death was even in their woollen jumpers, each knitted to their own designs so their widows could identify their remains after a pounding by the waves. They were not callous like the Ormeshadowers; they came to pay their respects as though this were one of their own, as if they owed these women an apology on behalf on the errant ocean for stealing a husband who wasn't hers to take.

One of them stepped forward. He was young, the colour high on his cheeks. He held his cap over his heart.

"I'm Michael Piercy. Ambrose Martin, over there, found him down by the Orme."

Ambrose Martin dragged his eyes off the table set with grief.

"He tried to speak to me."

Michael Piercy shook his head.

"Hush, Ambrose," he said gently, "you'll upset these nice ladies. Begging your pardon, but he couldn't have been alive when he found him. What Ambrose heard was probably the rumbling the dead make afterward . . ."

His voice trailed off. Maud nodded. The fishermen did not have the only claim on the mysteries of death. The villagers knew them too. The birthing bed could easily become the deathbed. Death lived in their cottages and fields. It rattled in their chests in winter and glowed in the fever-slapped faces of their children.

Neither John nor Thomas Belman had been home in the last four days. They'd searched for them in ditches and brooks. They searched on the distant hills, where the streams looked like silver ribbons. They searched on the Orme. They knocked on doors, only to be met by the pinched faces of the Ormeshadow villagers who said they knew nothing. Finally a search party was organised and Maud went to the valley to see if there was news.

Maud recognised death, even when it wouldn't show its face.

Ambrose Martin, the fisher of men, started to weep.

~

The children loitered in the yard, none sure who was fatherless. Samuel and Gideon circled each other, uncertain of what to do. Charity jumped in puddles, breaking up the clouds that drifted in them. Peter strolled aimlessly, avoiding his sister's muddy splashes.

"I don't care if it's my father." Recently Peter felt he had to challenge the older boys, even when he knew it would earn him a clout.

"What a wicked thing to say." Gideon was first to respond.

"Don't care," Peter replied.

"Don't care, don't care," chanted Charity.

"Shut up. All of you just shut up." Samuel kicked at the wall of the farmhouse. "I'm going to look."

They followed, sidling up to the window. Charity squirmed to get between them, even though she was too short to see in. They pressed their faces to the glass. Gideon wiped away their breath with his cuff.

The body still wore its impromptu shroud.

Ambrose Martin's arms hung by his sides, his hands too heavy to lift them and wipe his tear-mottled face. Michael Piercy patted his shoulder as if willing him to gain control of himself. Clare wrapped her arms around her own waist, like she needed comforting. Maud seemed calm, but her face was as pale as the linen on the body.

It wasn't unheard of for Thomas to go off. His dark moods came in fits and he righted himself by disappearing for days and drinking them away. The black broodings had stopped when John returned, despite his foul tempers remaining.

Gideon watched his mother and Clare look at each other as if deciding something. Maud was the braver of the two. She crossed herself and went to find out whose husband it was. In doing so she blocked the boys' view.

"What's happening?" Charity asked, receiving a sharp elbow from Peter in return.

Maud unwound the cloth covering the body. Gideon's guts twisted. He could see his mother's mouth fall open, her face full instead of its normal smoothness, and then she recomposed herself. Gideon thought, *It's Uncle Thomas.* His legs shook.

Maud went to Clare, who stood stiff and tall staring at the strange feast laid out on the table.

Gideon's legs gave way. It was his father after all.

~

The sea had bleached the colour from John Belman's skin, like driftwood left at the mercy of the tide for too long. Seaweed was knotted in his hair. There was dirt on his face, and his brine-soaked clothes had dried to stiff tatters. Clare bathed him with a rag.

"Gideon, come away."

Maud's gentle arm slid around him. He shook his head.

"I'm staying."

"You shouldn't see this." Maud stroked his hair, pushing it out of his eyes. Stubborn, he held on to his tears.

"I'm staying."

"Let him suit himself." Clare's voice was broken glass.

"Clare, I don't think that's wise."

Clare sliced off the remains of John's shirt with a pair of scissors.

"He's my son. Don't tell me what's best for him."

Maud slumped in the dragon chair. Mother Wainwright had asked her for help birthing Hettie's baby, while the eldest girl, Eliza, looked after her sisters. Hettie bore her child with a shocking stoicism for a woman widowed for so many years. Bad mother and bad daughters was the village litany as her belly showed.

When Maud had returned, the house was empty of men and all Clare would do was shake her head and say they'd argued.

"Thomas didn't kill him," Maud blurted out. She had wanted to be alone with Clare to talk. Somewhere away from Gideon and John, but it came out anyway. "He's a devil when his blood's up or he's had a drop or two to drink, but he wouldn't do this. There were witnesses to where he was."

"I didn't say I didn't believe it. The constable himself says he's been accounted for. There's no shortage of witnesses to where he was." Drinking, drinking away for days, fit to drown himself in the stuff.

"Dad knew the Orme with his eyes shut."

Clare turned her gaze on him. He looked like he was going to say something more, but she stared him down and then wrung out the rag in the bowl beside her.

His father had been found on the rocks at the foot of the Orme. Only a boat on the water would have seen him. Gideon had stood far above him, shouting for him over and over, but not seen him because of the steep angle of the Orme's face.

Clare lifted John's arm, wiping away the salt and dried blood. She frowned as she reached his hand. She went to his trouser pockets, but they were empty.

"His wedding ring. It's gone."

"It must have come off."

"No, it was too small for him. It was always hard for him to take it off."

"Do you think one of them took it?" Maud meant the fishermen. "Surely no one would do such a thing."

Gideon forced himself to look again. One side of his father's head had caved in from the impact of landing. Gideon's fingers closed around the ring in his pocket. He'd been too frightened to tell his mother. The longer he left it, the harder it became, until knew it was too late to give it to her. It felt so heavy for such a small thing. Gideon imagined falling from the Orme, the weight of it carrying him down and down.

He saw his father sitting on the Orme, in the dark, thinking. Did he run to the precipice or simply step off? As he plummeted toward the cold, black sea did he think, *This is a mistake, I want to live*? Was he afraid?

A word. Gideon could have given him another word, *Dad* called louder so it carried into the night to fetch him back. Or Gideon could have run out after him, his bare feet fearless on the cold cobbles. Or Gideon should have been brave enough to knock on his mother's bedroom door, the ring still warm from his father's hand, so she'd pull on her coat and together they would go after him and find him sitting there and hold him in their arms and say,

Come home, come home. We love you, come home.

Gideon could never tell her about the ring.

Such simple things to stop a man from taking his life; a pair of shoes or a word shouted louder or a boy's courage.

The Will

HENRY HIPPS, THE SOLICITOR from Bath, arranged to meet the Belman family at Carrside for the reading of the will, as he was travelling north to see his sister. He rented rooms at The Swan, known for its respectability and clean sheets.

Before the Belmans took the dogcart to Carrside, there were the conventions of death to deal with.

There was the cutting of a lock of John's hair to make a mourning brooch for Clare. Gideon watched Thomas do this with his shears before Maud had time to go and fetch the scissors from the sewing basket.

There was John's burial on the wrong side of the church wall, the minister turning the pages of his Bible with disdain as though he alone had foreseen John Belman would come to no good. There were the alms for the poor and the prayers for his damned soul.

Ambrose Martin, the fisherman, came to pay his respects to John Belman. The man hovered at a distance from the Belman family, wringing his cap in his hands.

Then there was the cleaning of the kitchen table. Clare and Gideon scrubbed it in salt and silence. It stung Gideon's fingers where he had bitten his nails to the quick and stripped the skin from around them. He was glad. Some feeling remained in part of him at least.

Then they donned their best clothes to go to Carrside.

Henry Hipps shook their hands in turn, starting with Clare.

"Mrs. Belman." Mr. Hipps bowed low. "I am sorry for your loss. I liked your husband very much. An admirable man. A sad day indeed."

Gideon's mother wasn't diminished by her widow's weeds. Gideon saw how men were taken by her face and then disappointed on seeing the wedding ring on her hand. Now, seeing her mourning clothes, hope glimmered in their admiring glances.

Thomas was clean-shaven. He wore his brother's best suit, altered to fit by Clare, with a mourning band on one arm. She was furious when Gideon had suggested his father should be buried in it. *A waste of good cloth. We aren't rich enough to be sentimental. You've been spoilt for too long.*

Thomas looked like a gentleman in his new clothes. Gideon saw his uncle was not all rough and ready, he could be as he chose, changing his bearing and character like changing his clothes.

"Mr. Belman, how do you do?" Mr. Hipps held out a hand. "May I offer my condolences and comment on the strong family resemblance of the Belman men?"

"Yes, Mr. Hipps, good of you to notice. My father sometimes mistook me for John and vice versa. My own boys are just the same."

Samuel, Peter, and Charity had been left at the farm with a list of chores under the watchful eye of Mrs. Phelps, one of the few villagers stern enough to keep them in check.

"It is a tragedy."

"Mr. Hipps, thank you for your kind words and sensitivity in the circumstances. This is my wife, Maud. Say hello, dear."

Maud curtsied with servility and confusion. Her husband was indeed in disguise.

Mr. Hipps turned to Gideon. "And you must be Gideon Belman! You're the image of your father. Very image. Sad, sad day. How old are you?"

"I'm ten, sir." Gideon's voice was rusty from neglect.

"And tall for ten. Tall."

Introductions over, chairs were assembled. Mr. Hipps had ordered a fire. The clock chimed the hour.

"Shall we begin?" Mr. Hipps took a seat at the desk. Clutching the bottom of his waistcoat, he pulled it down with a jerk.

The will was already laid out before him. He broke the blob of red wax with a snap and a jagged line divided the seal. The paper crackled as he unfolded it and smoothed it out flat with his palm.

"Yes, yes." That was all he said. He read on, with no further explanation, as though he were alone in his own office. There was just the sound of the clock and expectation.

Gideon looked out the window. Below, out of sight, there were chambermaids and stable boys, women on the street shopping for lace and men about their business. All these goings-on as if the absence of John Belman hadn't caused a momentous change in the world.

Hipps's bumbling was done now and he was earnest, with all his authority as a partner in Hipps, Fletcher, & Blaxendale.

"I, John Jeremiah Belman, of sound mind and body, do . . ."

When Henry Hipps read aloud it was in an unchanging drone with none of the inflections Gideon's father used. Whatever John Belman was reading from, be it even a list of errands or a book of myths, he made the words sing off the page.

Gideon made fists of his raw hands, dry from the salt and scrubbing of the table. He clenched them, stretching the skin until it cracked. He did it again and the crack deepened, blood rushing to fill it.

"... and to Professor Davies, my housemaster at Wainscot College, should he still be living, I leave the etching *David Slaying Goliath* he so admired, along with my deepest gratitude for all the kindness he showed me when I was his student."

The etching had hung in the parlour of their home at Bath. David stood with one foot on the chest of the fallen giant, an arm raised to heaven in victory. His father had not updated his will. The etching had been sold to help with the cost of moving to Ormeshadow.

"Finally, the remains of my estate, that is to say, my half share in Ormesleep Farm, which includes half the farmstead, land, implements, and livestock, I leave to my wife, Clare Elizabeth Belman. In the event of her death prior to mine, this is to be left to my son, Gideon Nathaniel Belman. There is one exception to this, however." Mr. Hipps had found it in him to raise his voice, making Gideon jump. "I request that the carved chair to be found at Ormesleep Farm, which was bequeathed to me by my father, be passed directly to Gideon Nathaniel Belman, along with the piece of land named the Orme, details of which are below. This also includes any items found on the aforementioned land."

Thomas turned his eyes on Gideon and fixed him with his unwavering gaze. Clare caught it and frowned, not knowing enough of Belman mythology to understand the significance of her husband's bequest.

All Gideon could think was, *The Orme is mine. The Orme is mine. She is mine. She is mine.* Finally, something resembling a feeling welled inside him, bitter and sweet all at once.

~

They ate before returning home. The dining room at The Swan smelt of beef and gravy. Maud shuffled in her seat and looked around, but Clare sat, smiling, as though she were accustomed to being waited on.

"Thank God," Clare said when the food arrived, "I'm sick of mutton."

The beef came as thick slabs, served with the potatoes, crispy from roasting in goose fat. Thomas ate with gusto. In company, at the head of the Belman family, he became effusive.

"Here, Gideon, have another slice of meat. You've hardly touched a thing. Eat."

Gideon put the meat in his mouth and chewed. He knew the beef was tender, but it had no taste. He wasn't hungry. The room was too full of laughing people and Thomas's false concern.

Gideon made a fist of his hand and the fresh scab

cracked open like the seal on the will, blood the colour of wax welling up. It was because of this that he was able to sit through the meal.

~

Thomas and Clare walked ahead, her skirts swinging as she matched his stride. Maud followed behind them, an arm around Gideon.

"Gideon"—Maud drew him close—"I want you to know I've never known a better man than your father. I am sorry."

They paused to let a maid with a laden tray pass as the corridor was narrowed by a pair of young women who stood talking.

"Oh, Martha, he has such a dignified air and she is so lovely." The young woman nodded at the receding backs of Thomas and Clare. "What a handsome couple they are."

Maud and Gideon passed the gossiping women, who had moved onto another subject. Gideon waited for his aunt to exclaim over the mistake and laugh, once out of their earshot. Instead her mouth became a grimace and they didn't speak again for the whole journey back to Ormesleep Farm.

At the Table

"SO YOU SEE, SAMUEL and Gideon must give up school."

Thomas sat in the dragon chair at the head of the table.

"I don't know." Clare was alarmed by this turn of events. "John wouldn't have liked that. For either of them."

Gideon stood in the door, wood stacked up in his arms. His breath was given shape by the cold air.

"Samuel is twelve and Gideon is ten. Not long before they're men. When I was their age I was working alongside my father."

"Sam has done so well in the last few years with John to teach him," said Maud as she lifted the pot from the oven.

Thomas sat back in the chair. "I wasn't speaking to you."

He said it so quietly that it made Gideon shudder.

Samuel and Peter had followed him in, carrying pails of milk and more firewood. Gideon could tell they too felt the heavy threat in the room and were quiet.

"It's like this." Thomas leant forward, his voice full of reason. "You own half the farm, but you can't work it."

"Yes, but you worked the whole farm yourself before we came," Clare interrupted him.

Thomas inhaled sharply. Gideon quickly finished

stacking the logs in the basket and grabbed the handle of the poker, pretending to stoke the fire. He let the tip lie in the white embers at the fire's core to get it good and hot as he kept his eyes on Thomas.

"Clare," Thomas sighed, "I'm not making any threats or trying to cheat you. When John came we made a heavy investment in sheep, there being two of us then to manage them. We planted extra crops. We've more mouths to feed. Don't you see? I need Sam and Gideon to help now."

She nodded, unable to fault his argument, but looked unhappy.

"And remember, the boys need to learn. They'll be running the farm one day, with sons of their own."

Gideon had never looked so far into a future that involved Ormesleep.

Clare twisted her wedding ring around her finger. "Could Gideon not stay on at school a little longer? Just until he's the age Samuel is now. Then they'll have had the same amount of schooling."

"How can I take one out and not the other?" Thomas asked as if the two boys were inseparable. "And I was taken out before John and felt it very keenly. It was as if he were worthier of lessons than I."

Gideon took off his coat. He was careful to hide his upset. His uncle's eyes burned his back. Samuel didn't care about school. He sat idle at the kitchen table. With John gone, he no longer read books at home and had gone back to killing things for sport.

"Oh, Clare." Thomas shook his head. "I'm running half the flock for you for nothing." Her flare of anger at this amused him. "I know you and Maud do what you can in the fields and you take in a little sewing, but the flock is our main income."

Maud cut the pudding. The meat and kidney inside glistened. She was angry. Gideon could tell from her jerky movements. She spooned out Clare's portion, slopping the gravy onto Clare's lap.

"Be careful!" Thomas barked at Maud, and she jumped. He tore up the bread and dipped it into his dish, the fluffy softness stained dark with the juices. He put the sopping bread in his mouth before he continued. "The only way I can see of sparing Gideon is if he finds gold on the Orme after all."

Maud finished serving and took her seat. Thomas hadn't finished with him yet.

"You know the story, don't you, Gideon? Your father did teach you it, didn't he, Gideon?"

Each time Thomas said Gideon's name it was a slap.

"Speak up, I can't hear you." Thomas cupped his ear in an exaggerated gesture.

"Yes, he did."

"What story is that?" Clare asked.

"I'll tell! Let me! Let me!" Charity had become bold and boisterous since starting school.

"Yes. Let Charity tell us." Thomas, the indulgent father.

"The Orme is a mountain of gold. And silver. And pearls."

"When have you ever seen a pearl?" Peter pulled a face at Charity. She reached over and hit him.

"And rubies. And diamonds and—"

"Hush now," Maud soothed her, "enough. Settle down and eat your supper."

Charity banged her spoon on her bowl and looked to see who was watching her. She was ignored.

Thomas took another mouthful of his pudding with all the daintiness of a lady.

"So with all those treasures Charity told us about, might we all not be better off?"

~

It was late and the house was still except for the soft knock at the door of Gideon's closet. Since he saw his father laid out in the kitchen, Gideon still imagined him there at night. He remembered his father's sticky, bloodied hair and the contour of his skull caved in on one side like an eggshell. He imagined the reproach in his waterlogged voice. *Where are you? Gideon? Is that you?*

He imagined his father's embrace. It would feel like falling.

The knock came again. "Gideon. Are you awake?"

It was his mother's voice. She knocked again. He ignored it, hoping to make her leave him alone, but she opened the door and peeped in.

"Gideon?"

She sat on the edge of his bed, even though it was cramped. She was immune to the cold, wearing only her nightgown, undone at the neck to reveal her creamy throat. She'd plaited her hair that day and now, let loose, it rippled like water around her.

"We've hardly spoken since your father—" She paused. "Since your father died."

He waited, not speaking. His mother rushed into the void.

"It's been very hard for me to be on my own. It's different for women than for men. There are certain hardships and worries we have to endure. When you're older I hope you'll come to understand. I hope you'll not look back and judge me too harshly."

Then after another pause, "I'm sorry about school. I know how much you'll miss it."

She took his hand. It was cold and dry.

"It's just the two of us now." She squeezed his hand.

"We have to look to each other now."

Still, he remained silent.

"Gideon, is it true? Did your father say there was money on the Orme?"

Gideon turned his face to the wall, pulling the blankets around him. He couldn't get warm. Her hand lay empty.

"No, Mother. It was just a story."

In the Ear of the Orme

"DAD, WHERE DID ALL the other dragons go?"

Gideon's father reached out and tousled his son's hair.

"Is that what you've been mulling over for the last mile?"

"No, I just thought of it now."

"Don't you ever get tired of dragons? What about explorers? Shall I tell you about Sir Walter Raleigh?"

"I know about him. I'd rather hear about the dragons."

"I'm glad"—his father nudged him—"those stories are my favourites too."

They turned their faces from the squall sweeping in off the ocean to steal their warmth. It carried rain with it. There was brightness and grey in the sky, all at once.

"Come on!" His father started to run.

"To where?" Up on the Orme they were far from shelter. The drops were getting larger, coming in gusts.

"Where are we going?" Gideon shouted again.

His father didn't look back, trusting Gideon to follow him down off the track. Gideon had to step sideways to keep his footing on the slippery, wet slope. Below them was a rocky outcrop, one of the dragon's ears. It was an upright crag, vertical stone slabs of different heights rising from the Orme. Gideon couldn't see how they could protect them.

Gideon's hair stuck to his scalp and rainwater trickled down his forehead and neck. His father stopped, pulling his coat over his head by the lapels. It was only when Gideon caught up that he saw the gash in the rock, just wide enough to admit a man if he turned side on.

His father grinned. "Go on, you go first."

It was a peculiar doorway. If approached from the wrong angle it couldn't be seen. The dark opening blended with the stone that made up part of the ear. The rock was thick with moss, soft against Gideon's palm.

The narrow entrance made it dark inside. Gideon had expected a damp smell, but it was dry earth.

"You never showed me this before."

"I was saving it. Take your coat off before you catch a chill."

He watched his father's big hands wringing it out, water running over his knuckles and dripping from his fingers. He shook the creases from the coat and laid it on a rock before doing the same with his own. There was a bulge beneath his

*father's shirt. It was a parcel, wrapped in oilcloth. It con-
tained a small knife, twine, and a tinderbox. There was a
bundle of twigs in the corner. The day had been planned.*

They bound the twigs together and lit them. The light flick-
ered unsteadily around the cave. It was larger than Gideon had
first thought, the rocks ridged and veined. The cave ran backward, narrowing and twisting into the earth until Gideon could
no longer creep along its length. It also seemed to get warmer as
it got deeper, as though heated by internal fires.

"She can hear you most clearly here. Every word you say
to her."

"Can she?" Something occurred to Gideon. "How do you
know she's not dead?"

John Belman touched the walls. "She's just asleep. Death
and sleep are not the same."

They settled on the floor, drawn-up knee against drawn-up
knee, shoulder to shoulder for warmth. Gideon's father stuck
the flare in a hole he'd dug with his bare hands in the soft dirt
floor.

"If she can live so long, what about the others?"

"Dragons are desirable and dangerous. The old armies
used to drink their blood before a battle to make them in-
vincible. They believed eating raw dragon heart could make
a man immortal. Dragon scale, ground to a powder, could
make a dead man rise and walk when sprinkled on his body,
and if drunk with wine it could turn back any poison."

"How could a man kill a dragon?"

Gideon shuddered with the cold and his father put a companionable arm around him.

"Everything can be hunted and killed. A dragon could be taken down with enough men and nets. A well-placed sword or spear can kill anything that lives and breathes.

"If Gideon Bellamans had a mind to kill the Orme while she slept he could have been a very rich man. But her father had chosen well. In Gideon's care, in this remote place, she was safe. By the time the village had sprung up she had grown a skin of dirt and grass and had been forgotten."

"So all the dragons were hunted until they disappeared?"

The flare softened his father's face.

"The dragons have all gone, son. Not just because of us. Sickness can bring everything low, no matter how mighty. And don't forget that dragon killed dragon."

"But surely, if she could survive there must be more out there, somewhere?"

Gideon's sadness was in his voice.

"It troubles you, doesn't it?"

"When she wakes up, she'll be all alone."

"Maybe in some hidden place there's another sleeping dragon waiting for her."

"I hope so," Gideon replied with all his heart.

There was a gentle rumbling. The Orme was moved, somewhere deep inside.

"Does Uncle Thomas know about this place?"

"Our father used to bring us both up here, but Thomas never liked it much. He wanted to be off on the hills with the flocks and his dogs. I found this by chance. I don't think even my dad knew about it, so I doubt Thomas does."

Gideon nodded, satisfied. The flare gutted. It was dying, leaving only the thin grey light from the narrow stone doorway. They kicked dirt over the embers with their feet and sat in the half light, listening in silence to the music the rain made.

~

Gideon lay in the Orme's ear, wrapped in his bundle of rags, listening to the sad, soft drumming of the rain. He held his father's wedding band in his palm. It was warm and smooth. He was afraid that one day his mother would find it and he'd have to explain himself. That he'd have to give it to her.

Gideon went as far into the cave as he could and flung the ring into the narrow darkness. He waited, listening for the sound of its landing, but none came.

He wasn't throwing it away. He was giving it to the Orme, giving her a gift of the most precious thing he had.

The Dog and the Bone

GIDEON COULD SEE THE lamp in the kitchen window of Ormesleep Farm. It was no more than a speck because he was far off, up on the road. He left the top field because the light was dying, making his task of clearing stones impossible. He'd made cairns of them around the field's perimeter.

He walked the final stretch surrounded by darkness, keeping his eyes fixed on the lights of the farmhouse. Gideon had always considered the night a silent, empty thing, but since his father's death he realised it was full. There were noises or movements, part concealed in shadow, which disappeared when he turned toward them.

The wind had picked up into great gusts that buffeted him along. As it swept through the coarse grass it sounded like some unseen thing stalking Gideon, rushing along on its belly.

He wished Samuel had been well enough to come with him. Clearing the field was a job for two. Maud had sat on Samuel's bed that morning, with Thomas stood over them. Samuel's eyes were shiny and there was a fire beneath his cheeks. The fever made him rave and thrash about. His hair was plastered to his forehead and he smelt sour. Then the retching started.

Even Thomas looked worried.

What if Samuel had died while Gideon had been up in the field? What if Samuel was hiding in the grass, waiting to punish him for his selfish thoughts? His cousin would haunt him, propelled along on jerking limbs. Samuel's mouth would be an open cavern, dark beneath his gauzy shroud. His croaky, thin voice damning Gideon to hell.

Gideon looked about him, but all he saw were the waves of grass, rippling in the moonlight. He pulled his muffler close around his neck. It was woollen, a gift to his father one Christmas. His father.

Why didn't you call out to me, son? Why didn't you chase after me and bring me back to safety?

It was no longer his father, secretary and farmer, teller of stories, but John Belman with his head caved in. John with his bruised body. John with his fingers nibbled by fishes as they'd trailed in the water. John come back from his sinner's plot, soil still in his mouth and nostrils. Back to Ormesleep and his family. Back to find Gideon.

Why didn't you save me?

John crawling through the long grass toward him, with a kiss full of dirt and darkness.

Gideon heard a scurrying sound and looked behind him. There were too many clouds blowing in now, blocking out the moon. No prospect of light. The blackness was complete. Not a piece was missing.

Gideon fled. The road was uneven and when he stumbled he put out his hands to break his fall, using them to push off again without pause. His muscles complained at the sudden exertion, but he knew he mustn't stop. He knew he mustn't look back. Not at any price.

He ran into the yard, only allowing himself a backward glance as he wrenched open the door. The night looked back at him. Gideon's chest heaved as he leant against the slammed kitchen door as though he were trying to keep something out.

The devil hadn't followed him in. He was already there, sat in the dragon chair like a king, eating his supper.

"What's wrong with you?" Thomas stared at him.

"Nothing." Gideon gulped air. "I'm well."

He normally avoided Thomas. Since his father's death he felt as though he'd shed a skin which left him exposed to every insult. "How's Samuel?"

"Better. Maud and your mother are with him." Thomas tore a piece of bread in half. "Is it done?"

Gideon felt cold, despite the race he'd run. Rubbing his hands together, he went to the fire. Nancy was stretched out on the hearth, glorying in the warmth on her belly.

"I asked if you'd finished."

"Nearly." Gideon looked into the flames. He was in

hell after all.

"What do you mean, nearly?"

"The light was going. I couldn't see my hand before my face."

"What have you been doing all day? You'd better take your breakfast up there tomorrow and finish the job. I need to start ploughing."

It would mean another morning of Thomas hammering on his door. If he wasn't up straight away, Thomas would be at him with a clip around the ear and "Get up, you idle little sod." There would be a long walk, the weak sun slowly burning off the morning fog. The horses in Appleby's field would be steam and silver outlines. Beads of moisture clung to his coat and eyebrows. The earth would be cold as he dug out the stones so they wouldn't slow or break the plough.

Gideon washed his hands. They didn't seem his own. The chewed nails were torn off low down, making them throb. They were cracked and bleeding from hauling the rocks. The heels of his palms were scuffed to bloody abrasions from his fall.

He dried them.

"Eat. Your mother left out your share."

Gideon took his seat at the end of the table and lifted the lid off the bowl. He didn't care it was his mother's cooking or that it was lukewarm. His hand shook as he lifted the spoon.

The stew was as thin as water, and Clare's seasoning was careless. As it had cooled grease formed a thin rim at the edges of the bowl. It coated the roof of Gideon's mouth. Pale chunks of potato bobbed around. He fished for meat and was rewarded with a few pieces that had settled on the bottom. The fibres of mutton were soft, for which he was grateful. He shut his eyes, feeling lightheaded.

When he opened them, Thomas's face was made kind by a smile. He had drained his lot, keeping the meat for last. Gideon could see Clare had given him plenty. Thomas picked up a portion between his forefinger and thumb, nibbling at it. Gideon watched him strip the meat and the fat from the bone. When he realised he was staring, he went back to his own share.

Thomas finished, stretching out both arms. The dragon chair scraped the floor as he stood up.

"I'm done in, lad."

Gideon looked hopefully at the untouched second bone remaining in his uncle's dish. It was rich in pickings. Thomas made a series of clicking sounds with his tongue, and Nancy's ears stood up.

"Here, girl, you've earned it. You worked hard today."

He flung the bone to the dog and it fell between her paws. She started to salivate, her eyes flicking between the feast and her master. Gideon was salivating too.

Thomas smiled, well pleased. It was only as his feet were on the stairs that he whistled. Nancy set on the gift, her tail thumping in gratitude.

"Don't stay up late, Gideon," Thomas called, "you've a busy day tomorrow."

The Pugilists

"A DELIVERY FROM MY aunt." Gideon stood on the doorstep offering up the basket.

"Come in." Eliza Dorcus wiped her hands on her apron, delight on her face.

Gideon stamped his boots to clean them. Two-faced Janus had brought sunshine and snow. The flurry of whirling snowflakes in the night had cleansed the sky, leaving it startling blue. Walking across the pristine fields to Eliza's, Gideon was in a world made anew. Ice in the wheel ruts looked like glass. There was silver on the bare boughs. The air was so fresh it hurt his insides when he took a breath. Snow absorbed the morning sounds. The silence and calm glittered inside him. He wanted to share it with Eliza, to take her by the hand and lead her out into the glory of the day, but instead he took the feeling with him into the kitchen.

"Don't be standoffish. Sit down."

Eliza unpacked the gifts at the table. There were some potatoes and onions from the root cellar, some of Maud's famous bread, and a pat of butter. Eliza sliced off the crust and spread it with the yellow butter. She took a bite, her face dimpled in pleasure. Gideon liked watching her eat. She savoured each mouthful, her white teeth sinking into the thick slice.

"Where are your mother and sisters?"

The girls no longer went to school.

"My mother's taken them to Carrside. To the wigmakers."

There was money in hair. Eliza had sold hers first. She'd explained to Gideon how the wigmaker, Mr. Nicholls, had sniffed at her head and pronounced it sweet, asking her what herbs she used to rinse her hair with. How he'd handled it as though it were already on his workbench.

"Do you regret cutting your hair?" Gideon asked.

"Regret is for people who can afford it."

Gideon knew that for someone so poor, beauty was a heavy burden. He saw how the villagers looked at Eliza, like something spoiled after she birthed a dead baby out of wedlock, but men stood close to her when they could, casually touching her if they thought they were unwatched.

"Don't you like it, Gideon? I feel lighter." Without its

full weight, her hair sprang into fetching curls around her face.

"It's as lovely now as it was before."

"The robin came again this morning." Gideon enjoyed her pleasure in the simplest of things. She saved them for him. "He was on the gatepost staring at me with shiny black eyes. Cheeky thing. I threw him some crumbs and you should have seen him hop, Gideon, it was so funny. Little hops with his feet together."

She covered her mouth as she laughed.

"How is it you're always so jolly?"

Eliza wiped her hands on her apron even though they were already clean and Gideon regretted the question he'd meant as a compliment. Eighteen. Unmarried. One stillborn baby behind her and her reputation ruined. Nursemaid to her siblings. Both her and her mother slandered at every turn. Eliza lived without hope and kept a tidy house.

"My father used to say never be bitter. Once you're bitter, you'll be bitter all your life. My mum's bitter. And I don't want to be like her. Not for anything."

She smiled at him, but her eyes were wet. It brought an unbidden thought to Gideon: *Sunshine and rain makes rainbows.*

"No. You're not bitter, Eliza. Never you."

"Nobody understands me like you do. How old are

you now, Gideon?"

"Sixteen."

"I think of you as much older." Gideon was head and shoulders above her, his neck and chest thickened by heavy work. "You're so grown up in the way you act, compared to Davey and Michael, I mean. And your Samuel." These were Ormeshadow's most eligible bachelors. "And you're the most handsome boy in the village."

The pulse in her neck, the smell of the dried rosemary hung over the stove mixed with her loneliness conspired to confuse him.

"Gideon, you can kiss me if you like," Eliza blurted out. "I wouldn't mind."

Her bottom lip was full and red. He imagined it between his own. A thrill of pleasure shot through him.

"Gideon, I've always had a fondness for you. Your aunt Maud means to be kind, but she pities me."

"She doesn't mean to."

"It's no matter. Everyone pities me, except you. You're the only one I can really talk to."

She put out her hands to him. Gideon was always hungry. For so many things. Always cold. To lie down beside her, just for a few minutes, would make him warm again.

If Eliza had learnt to bury her bitterness, Gideon had learnt everything has conditions.

"No, Eliza." Her dimples disappeared. He couldn't

stand her hurt eyes. "You are worth far more. Don't hold yourself so cheaply."

He had never seen a smile so full of heartbreak. The sadness dazzled him.

"But I am cheap, Gideon, or didn't you know?"

~

The snow was melting to dirty slush. The ice in the wheel-ruts had been crushed, revealing the dirt beneath. The frosted boughs were wet and dripping. Gideon walked into the yard of Ormesleep Farm to find his cousins hanging about. He wished them away. He wanted to be alone so he could think about the morning and how Eliza had made him feel. How her curls and tears felt against his neck.

This was the winter that Samuel had found girls and Peter had found God. It earned Peter his father's derision, but he took his strength from the Lord, walking around like a persecuted saint.

Now Peter preached from a stone slab by the barn. He called out to Gideon. "You should take care around Eliza. She's the lowest of the low. God will judge her."

Peter was careful not to be too loud in his denouncement, as his mother was in the house and might hear.

"She is a Jezebel. A harlot."

"Don't, Peter."

Gideon lunged at him and Peter leapt away, skidding on the ice in his bid to reach the house and the safety of his parents.

"He's right." Samuel had been watching.

Gideon flushed. "No, he's not."

"Yes, he is. Late Eliza is Easy Lizzy now." He gave Gideon a cheeky grin.

"Don't call her that!"

Samuel's smile turned into incredulous laughter.

"You like her, don't you? Of all the girls to be sweet on, you picked Easy Lizzy!"

"Shut up, Samuel."

"And who's going to shut me up?"

It was a challenge. Gideon was as tall as the older boy and they had yet to test each other. Gideon shrugged off his coat and threw it over the broken plough which was waiting to be mended, ready for the spring.

"She's a slattern, you idiot. Peter's right. And he's right about your father, too."

"What do you mean? What's he been saying?"

They circled each other.

"That he was a weak sinner."

"Shut up."

"A worm of a man who wasn't fit to live."

Gideon threw the first punch. As he did, Samuel

turned his head so it glanced off his cheek. He responded with a jab to Gideon's stomach. It took Gideon a second to digest the pain before it made him gasp.

"Come on," Samuel goaded, "or are you a coward like your father?"

Gideon went for him, head down. He caught Samuel around the waist, lifting him off the ground as he charged. Samuel rained blows upon his back. Gideon slammed him against a wall and Samuel slid down it into a heap.

"Your father was a rotten swine." Samuel was no longer playing. "He left us. He left us all."

He scrambled to his feet. Their fists flew, rage taking them beyond sense. Samuel's uppercut took Gideon's shoulder, making him stagger backward. Nancy danced around them, low growling in her throat.

"You're no better than your father. Weak and stupid."

Gideon kicked his legs from under him. He pummelled Samuel with his fists, not allowing him to get to his feet.

"You have no right to talk about him like that!" Gideon raised his hand again to strike. There was blood on it. It stained the sludge around them. "You've no right to talk about him at all!"

The rhythm of the battering was tiring Gideon's arms, but he couldn't stop.

"Gideon! Sam!" It was Maud.

Thomas stood in the doorway, blocking it with an arm to keep Maud back.

"Look at the pair of you!" Maud tried to get past, but Thomas sent her inside.

"What's all the fuss for?" Clare's voice came from deep within the kitchen.

Gideon continued to bludgeon Samuel even though he should stop, if only for his own sake. Thomas curled his lips at the boys.

"Samuel, get on your feet. I didn't teach you to stay down except when I tell you to."

Strolling over, he addressed Gideon. "And you . . ."

Thomas hit him. There was a flood of colour before Gideon's eyes and then the world went black.

Spring

THE EWE WAS ON her side in a bed of hay. Gideon watched her chest heaving with the exertion of labour. She was tiring, but now she had started there was no choice for her but to go on.

"Go on, then. Help her, you fool," Thomas said.

"I am," Gideon replied through clenched teeth. He waited for the contraction to pass so he could check her birthing position. As it was, the lamb was jammed, unable to go backward to the warm womb that wanted to expel it or forward toward the cold, stark light.

Thomas sat on a bale of hay, giving Gideon the occasional order, but mostly he just watched.

Gideon's shirtsleeves were rolled up over his elbows and his right forearm was slick with blood and birthing fluids. He tried again, this time feeling a pair of hooves. When he tried to seize them he couldn't get a proper grip, as they were slippery.

He took his necktie off, as he'd often seen Thomas do, and tied them around the lamb's ankles. He waited for the sheep to strain again, pulling as gently as he could to help her. The lamb wouldn't move, and Gideon grew afraid his attempts to haul it out would dislocate its legs.

"What's wrong?" Thomas asked.

"It's stuck."

"Any idiot could tell it's stuck from the way she's been struggling. What are you going to do about it?"

Thomas looked at him from under his eyelashes and Gideon knew he was alone in this. He explained his plan.

"Go on, then. But mind, if either die I'll count them off your mother's portion of the flock. She'll not be happy about that."

Thomas was stringent with his tally.

Gideon went to work. There was the smell of straw

and the lowing of the cows who watched the unfolding drama from the stalls. Samuel and Peter had been set the simpler tasks of minding the flock and the farm while Thomas and Gideon saw to the lambing.

Gideon ignored his uncle. He put his hand back into the birth canal, following the forelegs. The lamb was desperate for freedom, its haste making its predicament worse. Its head was bent backward instead of being in the natural birthing position of chin on chest, which would ease its passage. Trying to be gentle, he felt the entrance to the ewe's womb. The lamb's shoulders were twisted.

Gideon put his hand on her belly and could feel the enormous pressure of her womb's contractions. No wonder she was exhausted. The ewe had stopped struggling. He hoped she was conserving her energy for the fight ahead.

When he felt her relax, he pushed the lamb back toward the womb's opening, one hand on the ewe's abdomen to ease the lamb into a better position. He grasped the lamb's head and pulled, so its head was bowed.

"Come and check, Uncle Thomas. If I'm wrong, she'll run out of steam."

He meant the ewe. Soon she'd be too tired to push at all and they'd have to cut the lamb free.

"Get on with it yourself," Thomas replied. Then, less

gruffly, "You don't learn from being idle."

Despite his words, Thomas was now perched on the edge of the hay bale.

Gideon took the ends of the necktie, which was still attached to the lamb, to help her. Soon a black-tipped face appeared, the lamb's head pushing out into the world. Then the rest of it followed, slipping onto the straw.

Gideon fell back, laughing with relief and delight. His happiness was unguarded. "It's a ram!"

Thomas was on his feet too and together they watched the scrawny-necked, knobbly-kneed creature trying to find its footing. His mother licked away the torn membranes to reveal wet, soft curls. The ram bleated at her and she responded.

Gideon washed himself, working the sliver of soap into a meagre lather. He used the cold water in the tin bucket to sluice the blood and muck away, leaving him with goose bumps. He was exhilarated.

Spring opened herself to him each year with primroses and violets, releasing imprisoned tadpoles to race around ponds. There were shy wood sorrel and swallows, flaunting their V-shaped tails. There were the lambs, which he loved. The first memory he had of lambing season was watching his father and Thomas help them birth. They gambolled, they flicked their tails, they bleated and leapt. Why else would they do such things except for pure joy?

Thomas stood by his side and they watched the lamb suckling, greedy for life.

"Go on in and get your supper," Thomas said, then added, "it's a wonder you didn't kill them both."

The pleasure slid off Gideon's face. By now he should have been hardened to it.

~

Maud put the cooking pot in the centre of the crowded supper table. When she lifted the lid there were curls of steam that smelt of herbs. She served Thomas first, setting a brimming bowl before him, then herself and her own children, leaving Clare and Gideon until last.

Gideon frowned. Maud normally had a good appetite, despite being scrawny. Today her own portion was small and she stirred it often, barely putting the spoon to her mouth. Instead she concentrated on the bread, leaving it dry instead of dipping it into the broth.

Charity was the only one who couldn't bear the silence. She swung her legs until Peter kicked her.

"Father, may I go and see the lambs after, please?"

Charity knew to be meek when talking to her father.

"Yes, of course. Your mother will take you." Then to Maud, "She can look, but don't let her pet them, not tonight, especially the new one."

"I'm tired. Let Peter do it."

Charity looked at her father, unsure if this was disobedience or not.

"And why are you so very tired, Maud?" Thomas asked smoothly. "You've been unwell all week. Tomorrow we'll need your help."

"Gideon's more than capable. You said so yourself. You told me how he managed the stuck lamb like a real farmer."

Gideon couldn't help but look up. Uncle Thomas was scowling.

"Don't give him ideas, Maud. He'll get above himself."

"Charity's old enough to go herself and do as she's told, Thomas. And I won't be helping tomorrow."

"Why not?" Thomas stared at her, the bread he clutched now flattened in hand.

Gideon rushed each mouthful, swallowing the bread and vegetables half chewed. He had no intention of leaving an unfinished bowl of food should Thomas erupt.

Maud had put down her spoon. She drew back her shoulders. "Thomas, I won't."

"Are you ill?" Clare looked from one face to the other, stirring her soup, always stirring.

"I'm tired because I'm pregnant."

Gideon watched his mother's eyes widen and then narrow. She shot a look at Maud and then Thomas, like they'd been plotting against her. Thomas seemed to enjoy the drama. He took in their astonished faces as he threw back his head and roared with laughter.

~

Clare and Gideon cleaned the plates. From the kitchen window the world outside looked vivid and unreal. Gideon could see the honey-coloured moon stuck low on the dark sky, like a puppet show backdrop he remembered from a long time ago. He wasn't sure if it was something he'd imagined.

He could hear floorboards creaking above them as Maud and Thomas moved around their bedroom. Gideon tried to tell his mother what it was like in the barn; the life he'd delivered from death, the life he held in his arms for a moment and then set free.

There was smashing as Clare slammed down Maud's best china jug. It lay in blue and white shards at the bottom of the sink.

"For heaven's sake, what are you talking about?"

"Why are you so cross?" Gideon was irritated. Her moods were as unpredictable as Thomas's. "Aren't you pleased for them?"

Clare turned on him.

"You're a dolt. Just like your father." She couldn't have

hurt him more. "Don't you understand? It's one more mouth to feed. And Maud will expect me to do all the heavy chores alone. You never think, do you? We're servants. Less than servants."

"Half the farm is yours."

"At what cost?" Clare hissed. "I hate it here. I never wanted to come here. This was all your father's fault."

"Then why don't we leave?" Gideon's voice was all quietness and common sense. Just like his father's.

Clare threw down the rag she'd been clutching and looked at him as though the thought had never occurred to her before.

"I wonder what he'd do if he thought I was leaving?"

Mr. Hipps Comes Calling

GIDEON KNEW SOMETHING WAS wrong when he saw the fine gelding tethered in the yard. Its chestnut coat gleamed. Gideon stopped outside the open kitchen window. The sweet stench of flowers from inside was so strong that it made him giddy. He submerged himself in the thick ivy, keeping as still as he could so as not to draw the eyes within.

His mother was holding an armful of lilies, the huge bouquet bound with pink grosgrain ribbon.

"Mr. Hipps, they're beautiful."

"They're from Lady Jessop's hothouse in Bath. Such rare beauty."

Mr. Hipps wasn't looking at the flowers, Gideon noticed. Gideon's mother had on her best dress and had piled her hair up and fastened it with pins. When she got up to put the flowers in water, Gideon shrank back, but she didn't see him.

"How are you, Mrs. Belman?"

"You see my life. Living here cured any romantic notions I had of idyllic country life. I make the best of it that I can."

"How is your fine son?"

"Without John here he has had to give up his schooling to help run the farm."

That his mother hesitated over his father's name made Gideon's throat tighten. It had been so long since he had heard it spoken aloud.

"Such a tragedy if he's as clever as his father was, and I have no doubt he is."

"Our circumstances have much altered. Without good influence and proper example he is becoming rough and wayward."

"Does Thomas not offer Gideon guidance?"

Clare didn't answer, her lips pinched together as if she were the model of discretion.

"Oh. I see." Mr. Hipps clutched his lapels. "When you wrote seeking advice regarding your situation here I was concerned. And glad. A lady without protection should not have to rely on strangers for help. I mean, I hope you don't regard me as a stranger."

"That you should travel all this way for such a trifling matter as my concerns about land boundaries is too kind."

"My apologies if my letter wasn't clear." He took a deep breath. "I'm here on a personal matter, not just in a professional capacity."

"How so, Mr. Hipps?"

Gideon knew his mother well enough to see her suppressed satisfaction and mock surprise.

"Mrs. Belman, would you do me the honour of calling me Henry?"

"Henry." She didn't reciprocate.

"Your husband's business has been settled for many years now, so it would not seem that I would be unduly influencing you."

"In what?"

"May I speak frankly?"

"Please do."

"Your letters have given me hope. Hope of things I thought long past in my life. I would be honoured if you would agree to be my wife."

Gideon clutched the ivy in his fists.

"Henry, this is so unexpected."

"I have a passion for you." Gideon couldn't imagine how someone like Mr. Hipps could be unmanned. "From the first day I saw you, I've thought of none but you for all these years. Your letter came as if from heaven. I would make a home for you and Gideon. I would provide him an education to make his father proud. And for you, Clare, for you there would be the best of everything."

"Mr. Hipps!"

He threw himself on the floor before her, hands clasping her knees.

"Do not spurn me yet! Let me have hope. Give me the chance to win you."

Gideon couldn't watch anymore. He had to intervene. Whether it was to save his mother or Mr. Hipps, he couldn't say. He opened the kitchen door and announced himself by dropping the empty pail on the floor. Mr. Hipps struggled to his knees.

"Gideon, dear lad, hello."

"Mr. Hipps."

"You've become a man since I last saw you. I've just asked her to consider my proposal of marriage, but I see I've made an error. I should've asked your permission first."

Gideon searched his face for signs of mockery but found none.

"No, you should have asked *me* first."

Thomas cast a shadow over the kitchen. His shirtsleeves were rolled up over his elbows, revealing muscled forearms, dirty from the day. He was flushed and breathless.

Gideon had seen Maud earlier, waddling away from the farmhouse, clutching her pregnant belly. She must've been off to fetch Thomas, alarmed by the solicitor's arrival. No doubt Thomas had left her to labour back up the hill behind him.

"Mr. Belman, if you feel I was beholden to you to ask . . ."

"I damn well do!" Thomas slammed a fist on the table.

Gideon was impressed that Henry Hipps didn't flinch but continued with contempt, "As I was saying, if you feel I was beholden to you to ask for your sister-in-law's hand, I apologise. You must see I hold Mrs. Belman in the highest regard and would be honoured if she were to accept me."

He drew himself up and turned to Gideon. "I can't replace your father. He was an excellent man. Excellent. What I would like to do is offer you my guidance and the education you've been missing."

Gideon had forgotten there was a world beyond Ormesleep, beyond Ormeshadow. Beyond the shelter of the Orme.

"I've yet to accept, Thomas." Clare glided to Mr. Hipps's

side. "Surely you can see the sense in my considering his proposal. After all"—she bowed her head—"with the baby coming I can't imagine myself wanted here."

Thomas looked like he might strike her. Gideon supposed he was angry as she full well knew with Maud's imminent confinement she would be needed all the more.

"I am grateful to you, Henry"—she turned to her would-be suitor—"but I need time to consider your offer."

Mr. Hipps kissed her hands. "My dear lady. Dear, dear lady."

Thomas stood over them, deflating.

Mr. Hipps turned at the door. "I await your letter, Mrs. Belman. And you, Mr. Belman, abuse your position. Your brother was a gentleman. *You* are not."

"Get out of my house before I thrash the life out of you."

Gideon wanted to argue the legality of Thomas's statement but thought better of it.

The Celestial Tapestry

GIDEON WAS ON THE Orme. It was a clear, warm night. The sky above was the rich colour of midsummer, dark but not a sombre shade. The sky would be tangible if he put out a hand. It would feel like velvet.

This view of the world made him feel inconsequential, which was thrilling and terrifying. It meant nothing mattered, not that Thomas was getting drunk in the kitchen or that his mother and Maud were having a spat over a reel of lost cotton.

The more Gideon looked into the sky, the more he saw. The stars had the brilliance of diamonds. He remembered his father beside him, both of them gazing at the vastness.

"Aren't they beautiful? They'll continue to sparkle long after you and I have gone out. Do you see those stars? The ones that look like twisted rope." His father pointed upward. *"A little higher. Yes, those. They are the Entwined Sisters."*

"I thought they were Pegasus."

"Clever clogs. Not here. The Orme gave them a different name."

Gideon made a huffing sound.

"You've stopped believing."

"No." He paused. *"Yes. I'm not a little boy anymore."*

"I know." Gideon's father looked sad. *"But this is true. You'll find out, one day. The stars' proper names were given to Gideon Bellamans by the Orme before she slept. They were passed down, father to son. I want you to know so you can tell your children."*

"Tell me, then." Gideon didn't want to hurt his father's

feelings.

"The Entwined Sisters were born as twins. They had two heads and four hind legs, but only two wings and one heart. They spent their life earthbound, those two wings unable to carry their combined weight. As recompense they were given a great gift. The power of their linked minds and blood made them able to see far into the past, before they were born, and far into the future, long after they died."

"That's sad. All your stories about the Orme are sad."

"There's no sad or happy. It's how it is. When the sisters died, the dragons put them in the heavens to honour their memory. It was the one place they longed to be but had never been able to go in life."

Gideon turned his head. He felt something blowing on his face, like a gust of hot breath, but nothing was there.

"They named the stars for the best of them, those worthy of remembrance, and the worst of them, so they wouldn't forget the price of folly or wickedness. It's how they navigated, the same way men do to find their way over the seas. And look there. That bright star and all the ones lined up above and below it are the Falling Warrior. His nose is the bright one at the bottom and his tail is the rest, streaking out above him."

"What did he do?"

"He is the father of all dragons. He stole the secret of fire from lightning and the dragon's roar from thunder."

"Why is he falling?"

"Because everything worth having comes at a price."

His father's voice was thick with emotion. Gideon looked over, but he wasn't crying.

"What about those?" Gideon pointed to the north. He hoped the constellation would tell a happier story. "That cluster of six stars?"

"It's the Treacherous Brother. He was the most reviled of all the dragons. He deceived his noble brother and drove him to his death. He took his brother's crown, the queen, and cast his nephews into servitude, so he alone could reign and no one else."

Gideon turned away. The night was sour now. He wished he hadn't asked, because the words bothered him and he didn't know why.

"There's one last star."

"What?" Gideon asked, even though he didn't want to know.

"There are so many nameless stars that the Orme didn't think it would be wrong to take one for herself. Straight ahead, above the Falling Warrior, there's a single star. Do you see it?"

"Yes."

"Do you see how it burns with a steady flame? It doesn't flicker, because its heart is constant. It is for the Orme's champion. If he'd betrayed her when she was hunted by man and dragon, it would have earned him glory and riches. He *watched over her instead. She named a star for him. It's the Man of Honour. It's Gideon Bellamans."*

Gideon stayed out on the Orme all night. He woke, limbs jerking, as if falling from his dreams and plummeting into the dawn. There were dew-coated blades of grass under his hands. He watched the rising sun covering the Orme, burning away the velvet blue and the stars. He watched them go out, one by one. First the Falling Warrior, then the Entwined Sisters, the Treacherous Brother, and then, finally, the Man of Honour.

Michaelmas Day

THE RHYTHM OF CLAPPING hands and stamping feet shook the room, making the corn dollies, flowers plaited in their hair, jig on their nails on the wall.

"Why don't you ask Eliza to dance?"

"No. She likes Samuel better," Gideon replied. *Especially since last winter.*

"Don't be so sure. It's you she keeps looking at. You're a handsome boy." His mother gave him a sour smile. "For someone so clever, you're a fool sometimes."

"So if it's not her you slink off to see, who is it then?" Thomas had been slouched against the wall beside them but now straightened up, interested.

Gideon looked for a way to escape their scrutiny. Better Thomas think he was off with Eliza than up on the Orme.

Silas Day saved him by clanging a ladle on a tin plate. "Right! Be quiet, you rabble!"

Each year the villagers scratched their meagre bounty from the earth, bundling the corn into sheaths as it fell before the scythe. Gulls and revellers came over the fields to Silas and Mary Day's house, to the largest room in Ormeshadow. There they celebrated their hopes of surviving the winter. Each family brought a gift as thanks for the harvest. A pot of stew. A pie. A garland of wild flowers. A fresh-baked loaf. Old enmities were put aside for another time, or at the very least not spoken of.

The Belman contribution was a slaughtered sheep for roasting. Gideon had been shackled to Samuel by the carcass that they lugged over to the Days' house the previous morning.

The clanging ladle continued until the room fell silent. Gideon could hear the lamb fat sizzling as it dripped into the fire.

"Everyone grab a glass," Silas called.

The dancers dispersed.

"A toast! To Michaelmas Day!" It was Mary Day. "May we all be here next year to enjoy it!"

"Yes, you crowing old baggage," Gideon heard his

mother mutter.

The Days were merchants. One side of Silas was withered and contorted so when he walked he tilted alarmingly to one side before righting himself, as though counterbalanced. His mind, by contrast, was dextrous and supple. He was a born trader. A seeker and finder of opportunities overlooked. There wasn't a family in Ormeshadow that didn't owe Silas Day a favour, be it a half day of labour or a sack of something from their fields.

Mary was devoted to her husband. If anyone insulted Silas Day's manhood they'd be made to think again when they next came calling on the Days for a cup of sugar or a ball of twine. If Clare wanted a bolt of cloth now she had to go all the way to Carrside for it herself.

The dancing started again. Clare sat with her head held high like a queen, making herself more desirable and more damned. If a man put a foot toward her they were held back by the forbidding looks of their women, led by Mary Day.

Clare had deprived herself of a dancing partner, one who would have danced on hot coals for her, had she asked. Mr. Hipps's proposal had become common knowledge and Clare had threatened several times to invite Mr. Hipps, but in the end no such invitation was sent.

"Our revelries will be too provincial for the likes of him," Thomas had said. Clare had scowled back at him in response, but it was in good humour, as though he had made a joke. They were friends again.

Clare wasn't the only Belman woman not dancing. Despite being too pregnant to dance a jig comfortably, Maud had made the journey. She didn't lack for attention. Pregnancy had made a beauty of her. It tamed her hair and made it glossy. Curves replaced her angularity. Men stopped to talk to her and clapped Thomas on the shoulder as though he were liked. Women, drawn to new life, gave Maud advice as though she didn't already have three children. Many reached out to touch her belly as if it were public property.

Gideon picked his way across the crowded room, feeling the beat of the fiddler's arm. His heart picked up to match the pace. Eliza sat surrounded by young men, laughing as though they were telling her the funniest things. Desire swelled up in Gideon's chest, gnawing at his heart with its peculiar hunger.

"Eliza, will you dance with me?" Gideon feigned a boldness.

Samuel snickered, a nasty, familiar sound Gideon ignored. Eliza's eyes were pools of false brightness. It put Gideon in mind of something tarnished, something that could be polished up with enough love and care.

"Why should I dance with you?" Her smile was brittle.

Because I've never held a girl the way I want to hold you. Because my kisses for you would not be idle. My kisses would be promises. My kisses would be full of us.

"Because I want to dance with you." He lifted his chin.

She was hard. "I'll not dance with a boy."

Such contempt. Samuel lounged against the arm of her chair.

Gideon had meant to be kind that day, in the winter. Now he understood she thought him cruel. She'd mistaken his kindness for pity. His respect for rejection.

She no longer saved him the only thing, besides herself, she had to give. She no longer told him the details of her day, the first snowdrops or the breast of a robin. Things the other boys would have mocked. These last nine months of Eliza's coldness and sarcasm had just been her anger gestating, waiting for a chance to punish him. That must have been how much she had liked him.

If only he'd taken her out into the snow and silence. Perhaps then they might have understood each other better.

"Eliza . . ."

She pushed past him, brushing against him, wrong-footing him. Another body made contact with him, a shoulder jarring against him sending him reeling. It was

Samuel. Eliza was leading him by the hand to the centre of the room. The other boys nudged each other, hooting and gibbering.

Gideon stood on their periphery. The noise of the room was roaring in his ears, the music too loud for him to enjoy. There was a press of bodies and the cloying smell of spilt ale and roasted lamb.

Samuel's hands were on Eliza's waist, her hips, and the small of her back. She grinned and the watching women tutted. Already ruined. No better than her mother. The couple whirled about, setting her skirts swirling.

Gideon turned away, unable to look. He sought out the darkest corner of the room where they couldn't see him. He watched Samuel, whose attention was for his friends, not Eliza. With a wink, he flung her away into the arms of the next boy and the dance went on.

Armitage

"SHALL I TELL YOUR FORTUNE?"

"No, but thanks, Mr. Armitage."

Gideon wasn't alone. Armitage was waiting for him in the shadows. The small man's skin was wrinkled by foreign suns. Armitage had run away to sea as a boy and it cast him back on the shore of his birth as a man, like a piece of flotsam, full of scars and tales from his life on merchant ships.

"Just Armitage will do. Don't be standoffish, lad. People pay good money for my predictions."

"I don't want to."

"Are you scared?"

"No." Gideon bristled. Being scared was a felony in the Belman house.

"Go on." It was Mary Day, who had suddenly appeared at Gideon's side. She was Josiah Armitage's sister. "He has the gift, you know."

Gifts and heresies. In Ormeshadow there was no conflict between divining your future in a bowl of peelings and the psalms, or the collection plate on Sunday and leaving a bowl of milk by the door at night as a bribe to keep the dark at bay.

Gideon took a seat. He was more afraid of Armitage than any prophecy he could make. The man had a queer way of fixing you in his sights as though he could see right down to the bottom of you.

"Let me look at you."

The landlocked mariner took Gideon's hands in his own. The intimacy of it made him uncomfortable. He pored over the palms, examining them as though reading a book. Heart line. Head line. Life line. He turned them over, as if turning the page. He looked at the ragged nails.

"You've had a life of toil."

"So has everyone this side of Carrside."

"Don't get smart with me. And Mary, stop your eaves-dropping and fetch me some rum."

"You've had too much already," she grumbled, but went off in search of the bottle.

Armitage pulled Gideon closer. The noise and the smoke receded. He could smell Armitage's breath, the sweetness of the rum and sugar mixed with stale tobacco, and then beneath that the foulness of his damaged leg. Armitage's wound never healed. It oozed blood and pus from time to time. It was well known the surgeon said keeping it would kill him eventually, but Armitage refused to let him amputate.

"I've been reading charts and maps all my life," said Armitage. "This is just another kind of map. A map of you."

All Gideon could see were lines.

"A map is only the lie of the land. It can't tell me where to go or what to do with myself."

Armitage gave him a sharp look. "You hide yourself well, don't you? A man who doesn't want to draw attention to himself has something to conceal." Then he snorted. "You're quite right. A map is no use if you've no idea where you want to go. But think on. Some maps have the journey marked out for you."

He fell silent again, contemplating the direction of Gideon's path.

"You've been scarred by sorrow. Your heart is broken."

John Belman's story was well known. The bookish man who came back to Ormeshadow only to throw himself off a cliff. The story had carved out the contours of Gideon's face.

"You're a romantic." Armitage followed Gideon's eyes as they travelled to Eliza and back. "I don't mean just about women. I mean about life. That sort of romance causes the most pain, only most folk don't understand. You feel everything twice as much as everyone else. It'll do you no good. A big heart will drive you mad if you're not careful."

Gideon stared at his hands. Even now, when confronted, he denied the depths of himself.

"You look like the rest of them"—Armitage nodded to the stamping, dancing Ormeshadowers—"but you're like me. You don't belong here. The sea is my best love. Yours is for the higher things in life. Learning. You crave it."

Armitage cocked his head to one side. Their heads were so close that Gideon could see the pits scarring his cheeks.

"You must be sad to be here alone."

Gideon was about to say, *But I'm not alone,* but then he

understood.

Armitage put his forefinger to Gideon's palm, tracing out a line. The same finger went to his open mouth.

"Gideon, you'll remember me when the time comes, won't you?"

"I don't understand."

"I see change." Armitage pointed to Gideon's hand again. "Change so monumental it'll be as if Ormeshadow never existed. Once this part of your life is over, it'll never come again."

Their heads were together now, like conspirators.

"You'll be rich, boy. Richer than any of those merchants in Liverpool or London. A rich scholar."

"How might that be, you old dog?"

It was Thomas. He'd crept up behind them, stealthy despite his size. The two of them had turned from the room, but the room had been watching them. Armitage didn't tell fortunes for just anyone.

Armitage bared his remaining teeth at Thomas.

"Don't tell me, you see a dragon," Thomas sneered.

"Mind your own business."

"Everyone knows the Orme story"—Thomas paused—"and Gideon's disappointment in his fortune. Perhaps you could tell him where to look."

Armitage ignored him.

"Or shall we find it together? An even split." Thomas

came closer, demanding Armitage's attention. "No one could prove we found it on the Orme. Or maybe you're an old fake? After all, you didn't see that coming, did you?" He pointed to the weeping leg.

Gideon stared at them in horror, but Armitage shook his head.

"I wouldn't cheat the boy if I were you," the sailor said.

"Why?"

"I just wouldn't. Some aren't fair game. They're looked after." Armitage turned back to Gideon. "Remember what I said. Remember me when the time comes."

"A child's tale that's as real as dragons are." Thomas was reluctant to leave Gideon alone with Armitage now.

"Dragons are real." When Armitage grinned the creases of his face deepened to grooves. He spat on the floor. "I've seen them. In the West Indies." The dirty yellow glob of spittle landed at Thomas's feet. "They were the size of a fully grown bull. All tooth and claw and scales, with great forked tongues. And they could shift. We ran like the devil was after us."

"Did you see that at the bottom of a pint pot?"

"Why, what's at the bottom of yours? You're there often enough yourself."

Thomas laughed and slapped his thigh, full of mock mirth.

"At least I've no need to lie about where I've been for

the last twenty years. Merchant ship, my eye, you lying old pirate."

"No, you've no need to because you've not been anywhere, have you?"

Gideon recognised the look, a falling away that left a blank, smooth fury on Thomas's features. Armitage had wounded him.

"You'll be stuck here forever, Armitage. And I'll be right here with you, so you'd better mind how you go."

"I'd wish you to hell, but you're going there already, Thomas." He grabbed Thomas's hand and made a show of peering at it. "You'll burn. You're definitely for burning."

The Ship

GIDEON HAD BEEN SENT to fetch his uncle. The Ship stood by the road out of Ormeshadow, its lamps glowing orange in the low windows. The door, battered by salt-laden wind, was blistered and peeling.

He could hear the men inside, laughing and singing, coarse sounds that made Gideon pause. Without the influence of women, the men who danced on Michaelmas Day and who nodded as they passed Gideon on the road changed. They became unpredictable creatures once inside these walls with a few pints of beer inside them. Dangerous. Gideon wanted to run away, despite the hiding he would get for it.

He lifted the latch and went in.

The men inside were as worn and weathered as the door. Their faces were raw and male, stripped by sunlight and harsh winds. There were some Gideon recognised and some he didn't. They filled the cramped space with their tall stories and bravado, stooping where the uneven ceiling came down too low.

"Hey, it's John Belman's boy."

An arm grabbed Gideon around the neck and he was pulled in a headlock into the centre of the room. The arm restraining him was covered in rough serge that smelt of cheap tobacco.

"What do you want here?"

The voice was Jim Carter's, although Gideon couldn't see him. On the few occasions he'd come to the farmhouse at Ormesleep, the man had been all mealy-mouthed, referring to Clare and Maud as *the ladies*.

"I'm looking for my uncle, sir."

They laughed at him. Gideon tried to twist away, but he was caught like a rabbit in a ligature.

"Did you hear, Jim? You're a sir, no less."

They were a many-headed hydra, each one determined to have a say.

"Fancy man, just like his father was."

"He thought he was better than us with all his book learning."

"Scholar." The word was spat out.

"He was a secretary!" Gideon shouted out the words before he could check himself.

The hydra roared again. The arm gripped his neck tighter than was necessary, turning to show him where Thomas sat in the corner.

"Yes, until his master tried his luck with your mother!" That was James Collins, a widower who sat in the front pew at church each week, his head bowed. He leered at Gideon from his stool by the fire.

"What did he do, boy? Was it a quick kiss in the parlour?" Another voice.

"Did he put his hand up her skirt?"

"Was it while your father was too busy reading a book?" They were a chorus now.

James Collins wiped his eyes. "There isn't a man here who would pass her up, pardon my boldness, Thomas."

"No offence taken," Thomas replied.

Here at The Ship they could give full rein to their resentment without pretence at civility. Gideon's face burned at the insults to his mother and the way Thomas let them go. These men resented Clare, who turned their heads but was so far above them and whom they could not have. They liked that Thomas cheapened her.

It had been a long time since Gideon had thought of Bath. It was as foreign to him now as the places Armitage talked about. He couldn't remember why his father had said they had to leave; there were only memories of half explanations and evasions.

The heckling crowd pushed him away and he staggered head first into his uncle's legs. The laughter died. Gideon looked up into his uncle's black eyes.

"What do you want?"

"Mrs. Wainwright sent me. She says for you to come home. It's the baby. It's time."

"What for? That's woman's work."

Gideon was close to panic. Jessie Wainwright had been emphatic. *Make him come,* she'd hissed, soiling her apron with the muck on her hands. Through the partially opened door he could see blood and pain writhing around on a bed sheet.

Women. The weaker vessel.

"Please, Uncle Thomas, she said you must come now. The baby isn't coming as easy as it should."

"Did you not hear me?"

He knew from the fall of Thomas's voice that a blow was coming.

He'd not dare, Gideon thought, *not here, with witnesses.*

The crowd of men strained at the smell of violence. Gideon realised there would be no help there. They were eager for it to begin.

Thomas raised his hand and Gideon shrunk away, trying to stand less tall. The flying fist was stayed by the only man in Ormeshadow brave enough to take Thomas on. The Ship's keeper was as big as a shire horse and no one crossed him. Besides a thrashing, they'd have to walk the five miles to the next inn.

"Not here," said the giant. "Feel free to take it outside, but not in here. I don't like mopping up blood and teeth."

Gideon was hauled out of the inn by the collar of his jacket. Thomas flung him to the ground. His boot followed, connecting with Gideon's side.

Stay down, stay down, stay down, Gideon repeated again and again to himself. It was the secret of his survival. He could feel his own hands curling into fists. *Don't be stupid, he'll kill you. Stay down.*

"Don't you ever contradict me again, do you understand?"

Thomas struggled to lift the winded boy under the armpits, nearly losing his footing in the mud. Frustrated, he caught the side of Gideon's head with a slap that brought a satisfying trickle of blood from his ear.

"Do you know why I hate you?" Thomas's words sounded muffled to Gideon. "You've been trying to cling to Clare's apron strings for far too long. All you know are womanish ways. And you learnt those from your father."

Gideon found his feet. Still laughing at his own joke, Thomas shoved him over again.

Stay down, stay down.

"You're always creeping around. Watching us. You're no use to anyone."

Another shove. Gideon bit his tongue as he landed on his already bruised ribs.

"Do you think your mother wants you hanging around her all the time?"

So it was that Gideon went home, crawling before his uncle, to celebrate the felicitous occasion of the birth of a new life in the Belman house.

Discovery

GIDEON STOOD NEXT TO his mother, not in solidarity but because there was nowhere else in the room to stand. She didn't ask him why his ear was bleeding.

They were in Thomas and Maud's bedroom, a place he seldom had cause to go. There was a bed and a set of drawers under the window, on which was a chipped ewer and a basin. A mirror hung on one wall and there was a simple wooden cross on the other. The room smelt of sweat, blood, and milk.

Aunt Maud lay on clean pillows and sheets, leeched of all colour. The birthing linen lay on the floor, twisted and bloodied from the carnage.

Maud only had eyes for the baby in her arms who'd been hard fought for and hard won. It was red skinned and dry from being in the womb a week too long. Maud had fretted, wondering when it was going to come, until she felt the first sharp pain as she stood at the kitchen floor. Two hours later her waters broke. It was a torrent.

Such a little thing, with tiny fingers, to have caused so much fuss.

Maud's engorged nipple popped from the baby's mouth and it made a mewling sound as she buttoned up her gown. Gideon could see his cousins were embarrassed and he looked away too, but his aunt had never looked so radiant, so serene, as she did then.

"Samuel, Peter, Charity, this is your sister, Mercy." Maud beckoned her other children.

They crowded round. Maud had grown tired of waiting for Thomas to come up from the barn, where he'd stayed with Nancy while Maud heaved and strained upstairs.

Charity stroked her sister's cheek as if she were a doll.

"Careful," Maud warned.

Gideon winced when Samuel put out a hesitant finger and then jabbed Mercy in her face, making her wail and thrash the air with her fists. His mother reached over and slapped Samuel.

"Go outside and play." Maud ordered them out, as though they were still children who played with spinning tops instead of burly farmhands. Their descending feet hesitated as a heavier set came up the stairs. They scattered out of Thomas's way. Thomas ignored Clare and Gideon.

It was time for Mercy to be presented to her father. He took the child with no great care, making Maud lean forward anxiously, as though bound to the babe by an invisible thread.

"Thomas, I've chosen a name . . ."

"Hush."

He laid the bundle at the end of the bed. Exhausted from her long journey, Mercy had fallen asleep. Thomas ran a hand over her head, pausing to feel the life pulsing beneath the soft spot. He unwrapped the baby, noting the correct number of appendages. He appraised the baby, Gideon noticed, like he did a newborn lamb. There was no tenderness in it. It was all business. When he pulled the blanket back further, he snorted. "More damned women."

"Thomas."

He handed the child back to Maud and went out again. He had not asked his daughter's name.

Now, it was just Maud, Mercy, Clare, and Gideon.

"Our child. Mine and Thomas's," Maud declared.

Clare nodded, nothing on her face, unable to deny the truth in this statement. Gideon shuffled, the room too small, even though there were now only four of them.

"Here. Take her." Maud held out her daughter and Clare took her, holding Mercy away from her own body as though she were a bundle of canker. She laid the baby in the crib and started to pick up the soiled birthing sheets from the floor.

Maud rested back on the pillows, seeming satisfied with this at least.

~

Gideon could hear Nancy barking. It was sounded muffled to his damaged ear, as though he were listening underwater. He imagined her black-and-white face, nose to the ground, until she picked up Thomas's scent and fell silent. Excited, she would run to him and, drunk or sober,

Thomas would kneel down and make a fuss over her silky ears and let her lick his hands.

Nancy fell quiet. Gideon turned over in his bed, waiting for the sound of the kitchen door opening.

The low glow of the lamp Thomas had lit slunk under the closet door. Gideon held his breath. He'd had enough of a beating for one week. He sat up, fists readied.

Let him try it. Just let him try.

The footsteps were retreating. Gideon waited for their tread upon the stairs, but none came. There was still a faint glimmer of light, which meant Thomas was still downstairs.

Gideon shivered as he shed his nightshirt and dressed, careful to be quiet in the cramped space. A man fights better when he's properly clothed. Pushing the door open, Gideon winced at the betraying creak of the door hinges. He raised his arms before him, ready to defend himself.

He could see the dim outline of the tin bath on the wall, the kitchen table and the spinning wheel in the corner. The illumination came from the corridor beyond, from the door that was ajar. His mother's room.

Gideon crept closer, following the murmurings. There was a cry, like a gull on the wing somewhere far off, over the ocean, and then silence.

Afraid to look, Gideon peered around the door. The

bed before him revealed everything. Without his shirt, Thomas was less of a man and more of a beast. His coarse, large frame moved over Clare, back and forth, like a tide. Her face was contorted and for a moment Gideon thought she was dying.

If I died for you, would that prove how much I love you?

Gideon's black eyes shone in the lamplight. Thomas saw him, their Belman eyes mirrors, but he didn't pause in his attentions to Gideon's mother. Clare, by contrast, was lost.

Thomas took her hair in his fists. It spilled out between his fingers.

"Did my brother ever make you feel this way?" He was looking at Gideon as he said it.

"Never. No one but you."

He kissed her.

"Why did you want Hipps?"

"You know I don't want him. It was all for you. To make you jealous. I told you. Don't you believe me?"

He kissed her again.

"You're mine to do with as I please."

"Ssshh." She giggled, a sound foreign to Gideon. "Maud'll hear you. She'll sleep lightly now the baby's here."

"Do you mind her very much? Do I make it up to you?"

"Stop it. Don't talk like that."

She clutched at him, her nails digging into his shoulders.

"All the time you were with John, did you dream of me?"

"Yes."

"Are you glad he caught us?"

A floorboard creaked beneath Gideon's feet. He didn't wait to see his mother's face, unsure whether she would be ashamed or jubilant.

Flight

HOW COULD I HAVE *not known? How could I have not seen?*

Gideon sat by the road, panting from the run. He felt like there was an iron band around his chest, which made it hurt to breathe.

A hundred things, viewed through new eyes, made a mockery of his life. Furtive glances and whispers. The anger and coldness that fell around him for no reason, surprising him at unexpected moments. The confusion and the double meanings. The way Thomas, Clare, and Maud had kept their children unbalanced with random cruelties and neglect. It was how they endured what was between them.

Gideon played scenes over in his mind, examining the

evidence.

My father would have done this same thing. He would have stood crying as he imagined each infidelity and deceit. He would have stood on the Orme, one image after another bringing him closer to the edge. What finally sent him pitching forward into the darkness?

If I died for you, would that prove how much I love you, Clare?

Gideon went to his father. It was too late to save him, but he ran anyway.

~

The church was a brooding shadow on the hill. The trees that had been planted close together to provide shelter had been whipped into bent, gnarled men by the wind's onslaught.

Outside the holy perimeter was the plot for suicides.

Gideon sat by his father's grave, crying.

You knew and you still left me with them.

His mother didn't cry on the day her husband was buried. She watched, impassive, as they nailed his coffin lid down. Gideon's last view was the side of his father's head that was pale and perfect.

Lichen bloomed in patches of dirty yellow and green, tenacious in their grip on the rough headstone.

Gideon traced the letters. There was a name and a set of dates. No *Beloved Father* or *Beloved Husband*. The slab was cold and dead.

Sleep and death are not the same.

His father was not here. There was no cause for Gideon to stay.

~

Gideon ran to the Orme. The air crackled with dry heat, heralding the storm. It smelt of earth mixed with metal and rain. Clouds raced toward him, shadows on the sky. Then the deluge came, cold fat drops on warm ground. His wet shirt clung to him.

Gideon stood on the ridge, the tempest in his chest far greater. It howled around his rib cage, battering his heart. Arms skyward, he willed the lightning to skewer him to the spot. It came in fierce flashes, cracking the sky with cannon-shot thunder and letting the rain pour through. The rain rolled over him in waves and out to sea.

The storm didn't want him. Disappointed, Gideon lowered his arms.

He followed the path down to the head of the Orme, slipping on the wet stones. From there he broke away, travelling parallel with the coastline until he cut up toward the standing stones. Turning sideways, he slid through the fissure in the rocks and into the Orme's ear.

Gideon's wet skin felt cold and grubby, not cleansed by the rain. He was too exhausted to take off his sodden clothes. Instead, he burrowed into the pile of tatty bed linen and told the Orme his secrets.

~

There's a legend that there was once a mighty dragon that flew over the bay and swooped down to cool herself in the sea. She crept along the shore and came to settle with her snout in the surf, her great head resting on her forelegs legs as they folded under her. She shifted on her belly, lazy in the sunlight as it warmed her burnished scales. She sighed, emptying her nostrils of coiling smoke.

She slept for hundreds of years until long grass grew along her back and people forgot what rested beneath. A village sprang up in her shadow and still she slept on, until one day she heard a whispering. At first it was faint, but as she strained to hear, it got louder and louder until she heard it clearly, deep in her ear. It was a human child, a mere wink in time, where she was the slow blink that lasts for centuries.

Being long without company she came to love the boy

and waited for him to come and talk to her. The human tongue had not changed so much in the time that had passed and she understood when he read to her from pilfered books and told her about his father. When he was sad, it made her sad too, a single tear welling up and trickling from her closed eye. Sheep didn't drink from this sporadic spring, finding it too bitter.

She heard her boy crying in the darkness within her and she listened. This boy who'd never asked her for anything when she could have granted so much.

"Please take me away," he sobbed, "take me away."

She ached for her friend, who was now a boy made man by circumstance.

She'd slept too long.

The Orme shuddered, sending out ripples. She stretched, her muscles slack from sleep. In Ormeshadow, crockery rattled on dressers and coal dust from chimneys landed on hearths. Then there was a pause, in which the freshly woken wondered if they'd dreamt it.

Then it started. The vibrations grew stronger as the Orme fought to free herself from her partial burial in the ground. Wrought-iron bedsteads trembled and then shook violently as though possessed. Walls collapsed. Slate tiles slid from the church roof. Gravestones toppled. Horses bucked and reared in fright.

The earth was moving as the ridge of the Orme rose.

As she broke away, the land roared. It was the sound of the world being torn apart. The cliffs around her crumbled. Boulders crashed into the churning sea, sheep tumbling after them.

The Orme crouched, her claws scoring the ground for purchase. Then she sprang up into the sky, all grace and fury.

Those that ran out to see what was happening fell to their knees. The land tilted beneath them. The dragon above them stretched out her wings and darkness covered the wet dawn.

She wheeled around the bay in an ecstasy of flight and freedom. With each pass over the land, she poured a torrent of fire from her nostrils. Her flapping wings fanned the sparks and flames, making them leap from house to house, from tree to tree. What hadn't been claimed by the waves was scorched: the hovels and the houses, the church, the inn, the farms, and the very earth on which they all sat. The furious heat made wet grass into fields of fire. It was a furnace in which flesh melted together. Anything metal became molten. What wouldn't burn glowed pure white.

The outlying farms suffered the same fate. Ormesleep Farm was a funeral pyre. Flames licked the farmhouse and the barn had collapsed in on itself, becoming a bonfire of its own. It would be days before the fire died, black smoke pouring from its charred remains.

Gideon's Orme caught a current of hot air rising from the blaze below, letting it lift her. She climbed and climbed until she was no more than a black dot on the surface of the sun and then was gone.

Put to Sea

THE FISHERMAN, AMBROSE MARTIN, was dreaming of John Belman. It had been years since he'd found the dead man and taken him back to Ormesleep Farm. His dreams were always the same.

In the dream Ambrose found himself back there again, rowing toward the foot of the Orme, just as he had done on that day. The sea teased him, tempting his boat into more difficult waters. She was the colour of pewter, churning up white foam to mark the passage of the currents.

In the dream he could see the other boats, just as he had on that afternoon. Michael Piercy waved to him from *The Tern*. For all the other men's envy of his fine catches, they dared not follow him so far out. The sea was in Ambrose's blood. She gave him favours not shared with the others; silvery fish twitched his net, squids with their tangled tentacles and armoured prawns, like grubs curled up on his palm. She'd given him something more troubling. The gift of John Belman.

In the dream he could see the rocks around the Orme's head, like partly submerged sea monsters.

Ambrose Martin cast his net.

In the dream there was a change in the light, the sky becoming a fraction whiter. Then, just like on that day, he saw there was a man on the rock ahead. Ambrose could tell he was dead, even at a distance. His was so pale that his skin was translucent, like wet paper, revealing the blue veins beneath where the blood had halted in its tracks.

Why risk your life for a dead man?

In the dream, Ambrose rowed on. He looked down at his own arms, the muscles straining against the tide. The man on the rock waited for him, having all the time in the world. His coat was torn and his hair was matted with dried brine. Except for his colour, he looked like he was asleep. Ambrose shook his head.

Sleep and death are not the same.

The boat was caught suddenly and slammed against the rock. Even in his dream, knowing it was coming, he cursed aloud. His wife, Eve, turned over and saw his flickering eyelids. In his dream he jumped onto the rock and tied up his boat as best as he could, looking to check the hull was still intact.

The man's pale and perfect head was on one side, facing him. Then Ambrose saw the other side, which was all broken bone and brains. Then the dream and reality of that day diverged and Ambrose travelled down the stranger path, as he did with every dream. John Belman's eyes opened. Ambrose was never afraid. All he ever saw there was compassion. He felt himself loved without judgment.

The lips parted to reveal creamy, strong teeth.

Ambrose wiped the dirt from the stranger's cheek. He was cold. Immune to pain, immune to love, immune to life. Ambrose Martin felt something quicken within him, years of his neglected self. It flowed down his cheeks as hot tears. He would not leave the man for the gulls to pick at.

In Ambrose's dreams the man's lips were always trying to form words. Ambrose knelt down on his hands and knees and put his ear close to the dead mouth. He waited. All these years he'd been waiting, but all that came out was the rasping of air drawn over ragged vocal cords.

The words. If only he could hear the words. Ambrose waited, the jagged rocks digging into his knees, knowing there would be nothing but a terrible sound instead of the words that would free them both.

Then, the dreaming Ambrose Martin was surprised.

"Put to sea." The waterlogged words came again. "Put to sea."

Ambrose opened his eyes.

~

Ambrose Martin put to sea. Martin Piercy ran to the end of the jetty, calling for him to come back. The other fisherman shook their heads, incredulous as they watched him leave. The sea was still agitated in the wake of the storm that had destroyed Ormeshadow. It churned, not knowing how to settle.

Ambrose was moving across the bay toward where the Orme had been. She'd collapsed, consumed by the waves and the hollows within herself, and now all that remained was a sheer cliff face, great columns of fresh stone rising out of the water. The wind swept the glowing ashes of Ormeshadow out to sea, where they landed with a hiss. The sky was dark with smoking clouds.

The rock where he'd found John Belman was visible ahead. There would be a new landscape beneath the waves, fresh mountains and valleys, just as there was above it. There would be great chunks of the Orme on the seabed, waiting to puncture Ambrose's boat, *Cathy*.

It suddenly occurred to Ambrose Martin that he didn't

want to die after all. Instead of drifting, he put out his oars, but it was too late. He was already committed to the vortex. Then, as *Cathy* went around and around, taken by the current, he saw that the rock up ahead was not a rock after all, but a boy on a rock.

Ambrose hauled himself onto this arid island, tying up his boat as best he could. The boy had a full mouth, in the shape of Cupid's bow, and a square jaw. His eyebrows were heavy. His face was no less masculine for the long eyelashes.

It was John Belman all over again.

Was it sleep or death?

The boy's lips were dry and cracked. He had curled up on his side and waited to die rather than take his chances by plunging into the inky, churning water and swimming miles along the coast to the beach.

Ambrose knelt down and waited for the feeling of breath on his cheek. Unsure, he shook the boy's shoulders. Nothing. He shook the shoulders again, harder. The eyelids fluttered and then opened. The boy gasped. He clutched at Ambrose's sweater with a weak fist, trying to pull him close.

"What's the use of gold when you have no water?"

Then the boy laughed. It was a dry sound full of madness that made Ambrose realise he wasn't a boy after all, but a young man who'd had his fill of life and was already weary of it.

Ambrose looked to where Gideon was pointing. It was a hole in the rock. Treasures had been piled up in the hollow with no regards for their welfare. Gold, silver, and copper. Things that glittered and glowed.

A crown studded with garnets was tangled up on the hilt of a sword. There were caskets, worked in ebony and lapis. Coffers were broken open to reveal the coins they contained, flat discs of gold stamped with the images of long-dead emperors from distant lands. A rope of lustrous pearls so tangled that it was impossible to guess at its length. There were torques, once worn by chieftains who painted their faces blue before battle. Daggers nestled where they could, blades crusted with dried blood from the killing blow, while their handles were crusted in turquoise and ivory. There were shields and breastplates, marked with fabulous beasts. Unicorns, lions, griffins, and dragons reared up to vanquish their enemies, trampling them beneath hoof and claw. There were bangles and bracelets that once had adorned the arms of queens.

In the depths of this trove were gems, discarded like a child's forgotten glass marbles. They competed for Ambrose's attention, winking at him in shades of green and blue. Some were as clear and colourless as spring water from the heart of mountains. The jagged stones had been cut to make them burn from within, inspiring avarice and murder in the hearts of men and women.

A lesser man would have thrown Gideon in the water and loaded up his boat, but John Belman had chosen well. Ambrose had already found what he'd come for. He gave the king's ransom no more than a cursory glance.

He gathered Gideon in his arms, despite the dead weight.

"Oh, my dear boy, thank the Lord you're alive." Tears fell onto Gideon's lips and they were full of the sea and Ambrose Martin's sadness. "I did what he said. He told me and I did it. I put to sea. I put to sea."

The Journey

"YOU UNDERSTAND HOW TERRIBLE it will be?" Mr. Hipps peered into Gideon's face, anxious that he didn't understand at all. "Terrible. No one will think the less of you for staying here."

They were in the inn at Carrside, where Henry Hipps had rented rooms for them. Gideon's breakfast lay untouched. Grease formed on the cooling bacon. The landlady had brought it on a great tray, twittering and fluttering around the room, twitching curtains and checking the mantel for dust, and the two of them sat in silence until she left.

Gideon was grateful for Henry Hipps's patience with him. When he tried to say anything, it came out in halting, disconnected speech that made other people pause and look at him. His bruises were fading blooms of purple and yellow and his lips were still cracked as though he were permanently parched, a man recovering from a long illness that had made a brittle vessel of him. He could shatter at any moment and everything would pour out.

"I have to see," Gideon replied as though it were a solemn duty he would not shirk. He carried his grief close, along with the guilt of living.

~

Hipps followed Gideon at a respectful distance as he walked through the smouldering wreck of Ormeshadow. The ground was hot beneath the solicitor's feet and he wished he had hobnail boots like the others. Embers eddied like fireflies in the breeze. There were timbers reduced to blocks of charcoal. When Gideon glanced back at him, the solicitor was covering his mouth and nose with his handkerchief. It wasn't an affectation. The smell of roasted meat brought bile up into Gideon's throat, too.

Not everyone had been incinerated. Some were overcome by fumes and mummified in ashes. Men were identified by the gold teeth melted in their mouths or a woman by a pin that remained in the burnt rags of her shawl. A child by a bone that had been set badly after a fall from a tree.

No clue was discarded.

Where there had once been furious sound, there was now a listless silence. Men recovered the Ormeshadowers, shovelling the ash in silence. There was no calling to one another or singing to lighten the load.

Gideon rolled up his shirtsleeves to help with the bitter harvest. Afterward his face was blackened like a chimneysweep's. Mr. Hipps, unaccustomed to physical labour and in inappropriately thin-soled shoes, worked beside him as they cleared the debris of the farmhouse at Ormesleep. Everything was ashes, as if it had burnt hottest there.

~

The hallowed ground of Ormeshadow church had been subject to the same indignity as the rest of the village, so the deceased were carried to St. Barnabas, in the valley, for burial.

The trees around the churchyard were tall and sturdy oaks. Their roots reached out to clasp the dead, absorbing them in pieces and sending them heavenward through their contorted limbs. Ivy stole around their trunks and crept over the older graves.

Gideon spent nearly a morning there. Occasionally he'd squat down beside a headstone and stare at it in a silent dialogue. Sometimes he'd reach out and touch it in apology. Then, when his communion with the dead was over he sought out Mr. Hipps and found him by the Belman family grave. The slab was creamy marble with grey veins, its pristine surface chiselled with names. The solicitor had laid lilies before it, tied with grosgrain ribbon.

"They're from Lady Jessop's hothouse," he told Gideon. "I'm sorry. You must think me a foolish old man."

Gideon touched his shoulder in a gesture of comfort that made the man weep.

~

The Orme treasure had to be inventoried and packaged, ready for transport to London. An agent would be waiting, ready to arrange its sale.

"May I help?" Gideon asked.

"Are you sure? You wouldn't mind? It's a capital idea. There's lots of work to do. Lots."

Gideon and Mr. Hipps worked together in the crowded room, guards outside by arrangement with the local constable. Obscene wealth was piled around them in boxes, heaped under trestle tables and in wicker baskets. Each day they called for fresh supplies of packing crates, sand, and straw.

When Gideon first held a pen again in his calloused hand he faltered, spraying ink from the loaded nib across the clean page of the ledger. He glanced up, but Mr. Hipps pretended to be busy with a pile of documents.

As he made the list, Gideon's hand flowed, the pen moving across the paper of its own volition in a way that reminded him of the first time he saw his father take up the shearing shears to race against Thomas.

"Mr. Hipps. I don't want this." Gideon frowned, unhappy and inarticulate.

"Don't worry, lad. I can send for a clerk to help me."

"No, Mr. Hipps. I mean I don't want any of this." A sweep of his hand took in the whole of the room. "It's not right that I keep this."

"What will you do, then? Be a farmhand?"

Gideon shrugged. "I thought of taking to the drover's road."

"And then?"

"The hiring fair in London."

The drivers would soon leave from Carrside, hundreds of cattle hooves churning up the drover's road. There would be campfires and camaraderie. A night in London's fields, overshadowed by the city itself. Gideon Belman of Ormesleep Farm, of fabled wealth, would merely be Gideon, a driver's hand.

"Have you ever seen a hiring fair? No? It's where herds of young men have their teeth and hands inspected before their labours are purchased. They should not treat men so." Hipps put his pen down on the inkstand and folded his hands across his middle. "This has been a great tragedy. So much has been lost. Things riches can't buy back. If only one good has come from it, it is that you are alive. I can think of no finer man to wield a fortune."

"The fortune's cost is too high."

"You didn't ask for this. You have no interest in money for its own sake. You've been given the chance to make a difference in the world. A chance to help others. Don't be so hasty to dismiss that. Think of yourself as its guardian."

Gideon pondered the word "guardian," turning it over in his mind.

Mr. Hipps laced and unlaced his fingers. "You'll need

to finish your education if you're to manage a fortune."

Gideon moved on to the next tray that needed sorting. He raked through piles of golden trinkets with searching fingers as though they were no more than tin toys or glass marbles. As he tipped up a goblet, something rattled around inside and then fell out. He held it up, between his forefinger and thumb. The sceptres and swords were forgotten, pushed aside, along with other gaudy baubles.

"Mr. Hipps, may I keep one thing?"

"You may keep it all, if you wish! It all belongs to you."

"This."

Mr. Hipps blinked. Gideon was full of surprises. "Are you sure? Not a Persian dagger or a crown?"

"No, sir. This is what I want," Gideon replied shyly, palming the scratched and dented wedding ring, as though he'd found the greatest gem in all the kingdom. It was an oath, a pledge made in metal. A blessing and a sign.

~

"Stop the coach!"

Gideon had been staring from the window, the countryside sliding by. His face was suddenly animated, looking outward to the world instead of inward. He leaned forward, a hand gripping the window ledge.

Gideon climbed out and Henry Hipps followed. This was the last place on the high road from where they would see the whole of the bay. There were uninterrupted fields, falling away to cliffs and sky.

Gideon stared out to sea, searching. He put his hand to his eyes to shield them from the bright autumn sun as he scanned the empty horizon. There was sootiness in the sky over Ormeshadow that the sunshine couldn't dissolve.

The pale water between the ochre sandbars glinted. Boats bobbed on choppy waves, acclimatising to a coastline without the Orme. Ambrose would be out there. Not even Gideon's gifts of gold could keep him from the sea. No offers of a new boat would make him give up *Cathy*.

A wind picked up, making Gideon's shirt billow like a sail. It fluttered against his chest, but he didn't feel the cold. He looked out to sea once more. Then he decided he couldn't wait any longer.

Back in the carriage, Henry Hipps cleared his throat.

"Gideon, I'm not sure of your intentions. You'll come into your inheritance when you come of age, which isn't very long." He hesitated. "We agreed, out of respect for your parents, you would stay with me until arrangements could be made. But I'm of a different mind now. I'd like to offer you a place with me. A permanent place."

Gideon's silence made him hurry on.

"I live alone. I am unlikely to ever have a wife. It will be a bachelor's house. I would like to guide your education as I think your father would have wished. I would act as your legal guardian. And your friend."

Silence, still.

"I can give you a home, of sorts. A home."

"And what can I give you in return?"

There was no impertinence in the question.

"You will give me a future. I will throw open the windows of my dusty house. My heart will not be all withered parchment and memories after all. My life will have a new purpose."

"Mr. Hipps, I mean this with greatest respect. You will never replace my father."

"That's just as it should be."

Gideon allowed Henry Hipps his cherished myths of Clare Belman. He liked the man who'd come, postponing all his business, to be at the side of a boy he thought was a displaced, orphaned pauper. The son of the woman who had spurned him.

They shook hands, an agreement between gentlemen, talking of the future over the persuasive sound of wheels and beating of hooves, as the carriage bore them on. They were a good twenty miles from Ormeshadow when they passed the old gallows and Gideon Belman turned to Henry Hipps and said, "There is a legend that a great dragon flew over the bay and then swooped down to cool herself in the sea . . ."

Acknowledgments

A huge thanks to Ellen Datlow, who took a chance on *Ormeshadow*. It's an immense privilege to work with her. She's forgotten more about short stories than I have ever known.

Thanks to the team at Tor.com Publishing, including Ruoxi Chen, Lee Harris, Irene Gallo, Caroline Perny, Mordicai Knode, Amanda Melfi, Melanie Sanders, and Liana Kristoff. Thanks to Henry Sene Yee for his elegant cover design.

Thanks also to the editors who have believed in me, especially Paula Guran, Andy Cox of TTA Press, and Michael Kelly of Undertow Publications. It was Mike's encouragement that made me believe I was ready to publish a collection.

Michelle Noble has been my friend since the age of four. It was she who suggested that my scrap of a short story should be longer. Cait Taylor and Natalie Tsang read the early versions of "Gideon's Orme." Thank you.

Thanks to the Sharmas, Greenwoods, Kleiner-Manns, Kershaws, and Flannigans.

Meeting other writers, online and in the flesh, has

been a revelation. Thank you *all* for being so welcoming and kind. British Fantasy Con and Edgelit are my annual highlights. I want to say a particular thank you to Cate Gardner, Simon Bestwick, Julie Travis, Georgina Bruce, Carole Johnstone, Alison Littlewood, Penny Jones, Laura Mauro, Nina Allan, and Tracy Fahey.

And most of all, thanks to Mark Greenwood. Always Mark Greenwood.

About the Author

PRIYA SHARMA's fiction has appeared in *Interzone, Black Static, Nightmare, The Dark,* and *Tor.com.* She's been anthologized in many Best-Ofs by editors such as Ellen Datlow, Paula Guran, and Jonathan Strahan. She's also been on many Locus Recommended Reading Lists. She is a Grand Judge for the Aeon Award, the annual writing competition run by Ireland's *Albedo One* magazine. "Fabulous Beasts" was a Shirley Jackson Award finalist and won a British Fantasy Award for Short Fiction. A collection of some of Priya's work, *All the Fabulous Beasts,* was released in 2018 from Undertow Publications, for which she was a Locus Award finalist and Shirley Jackson Award winner.

TOR·COM

Science fiction. Fantasy. The universe.

And related subjects.

*

More than just a publisher's website, *Tor.com*

is a venue for **original fiction, comics,** and

discussion of the entire field of SF and fantasy,

in all media and from all sources. Visit our site

today — and join the conversation yourself.